HIS HUMAN PRISONER

AN ALIEN WARRIOR ROMANCE

RENEE ROSE

Copyright © November 2016 His Human Prisoner by Renee Rose

All rights reserved. This copy is intended for the original purchaser of this e-book ONLY. No part of this e-book may be reproduced, scanned, or distributed in any printed or electronic form without prior written permission from the authors. Please do not participate in or encourage piracy of copyrighted materials in violation of the author's rights. Purchase only authorized editions.

Published in the United States of America

Renee Rose Romance

Editor:

Kate Richards, Wizards in Publishing

This e-book is a work of fiction. While reference might be made to actual historical events or existing locations, the names, characters, places and incidents are either the product of the authors' imaginations or are used fictitiously, and any resemblance to actual persons, living or dead, business establishments, events, or locales is entirely coincidental.

This book contains descriptions of many BDSM and sexual practices but this is a work of fiction and as such should not be used in any way as a guide. The authors and publisher will not be responsible for any loss, harm, injury or death resulting from use of the information contained within. In other words, don't try this at home, folks!

❀ Created with Vellum

PROLOGUE

Lily flattened herself in the tiny washroom near the the old airship's controls. A scrape ran the length of her leg and her slave's dress had been soiled during her escape from her master's pod. She'd barely made it on the ship her fellow runaways had selected on the fly to hijack. A bead of sweat ran down her forehead.

Please don't let any being use the washroom before take off.

This plan had been eighty planet rotations in the making. It had been a miracle she managed to get out at the appointed time to meet the others. They'd chosen a day and a time. Picking the craft to board had been left to the chance of the day, but this one actually seemed to be ideal—a rusty old ship with just six crew members to overpower. She'd hidden close to the cockpit to aid in taking the pilot and first mate.

She peered through the slats in the door and watched him—a huge male of a species she'd never before seen—flick on the engines. A small, wizened female entered and settled in the co-pilot's chair.

Oh *veck*. Was she Venusian? If so, she would intuit Lily and the other slaves' presence on the ship. Venusians possessed extrasensory abilities.

The pilot initiated hover movement, easing out of the dock. If she weren't holding her breath, praying she made it off Ocretia without getting caught, she would admire his muscled shoulders, the bulging biceps and corded muscles of his forearms. He sat taller than an average human by at least a foot and his skin had a purple tinge to it. Two horns on the top of his head gave him a rugged, fierce appearance.

He steered the ship through the incoming traffic, weaving in and out at a speed that made her stomach lurch.

She closed her eyes and said a silent prayer to Mother Earth. If all went well, she'd be free in a matter of hours—a slave no more. Unless he heard about the other missing slaves, her elderly owner wouldn't notice her absence until late that night, and even then, he'd never suspect she'd made it to the dock and onto an airship. Ocretions grossly underestimated human intelligence and Lily had always played the simple, docile sex slave for him. Not that the old male had been able to use her for that purpose much. No, she'd been lucky with him. She'd only had to look beautiful in her scanty uniform and endure his petting while she served him.

The pilot punched up the speed, zooming into the outer layer of traffic, farther away from the odious territory of her captors. Traffic grew lighter and lighter until, at last, they made it into free space. The pilot set the controls and stood up.

"You should take care of the stowaway in the washroom," the old Venusian said.

"Are you *vecking* kidding me?" He cursed. "Why didn't you say something earlier?" He marched over and threw open the door.

She pointed her laser gun at his throat, but the huge male batted it to the floor as if she'd held a twig. Because it was too far away to reach, and his speed and strength greatly exceeded hers, she held her hands up and put on her best helpless female eyes.

"Please don't hurt me." She feigned weakness, knowing her beauty and slight stature worked in her favor. Seven years as a sexual slave had taught her a great deal about minimizing injury from males.

His brows shot up as he took in her appearance, and she knew what he saw. A slip of a human female, scantily dressed and possessing the qualities considered beautiful by most beings. Though she was used to inspiring hunger in males, the flash of it in his eyes came with particular satisfaction.

He was younger than she'd guessed initially—not much older than she, if she measured by human standards, but his eyes and the scars on his handsome face told a story of a life hard-lived.

So they had something in common.

She let the miniscule sex servant's dress she'd stolen to escape slip down her shoulder, revealing skin and the suggestion of one breast.

The pilot's eyes traced down, stopping at the place her nipple lay hidden beneath the cloth.

It puckered under his gaze. Her body's reaction surprised her. She never grew aroused from a male's attention, not even in the throes of sexual activity. Apparently purple skinned and horned was her type. Go figure.

"Oh no, pet," he shook his head, apparently steeling himself against her helpless female act. "You picked the wrong airship to hide on." After picking up her weapon, he grasped her wrist and pulled her out under the lights, giving her another head-to-toe sweeping glance. To the Venusian, he said, "Why didn't you tell me before we took off?"

The old female blinked her protuberant emerald eyes. She smelled of brownbeer and her short, black hair stuck up at all angles, as if she hadn't brushed it in days. "She means something to you."

His eyes narrowed and his gaze returned to her. "*Veck*. You know I don't believe in that excrement."

The Venusian shrugged. "Denial will not change your destiny."

He rolled his eyes and gripped Lily's elbow, steering her into the bowels of the ship.

She took note of where he tucked her laser gun in his belt, biding her time.

The pilot kicked open a sleeping chamber door and stepped inside with her. "What's your name?"

"Lily." She made her voice sound breathy, sweet.

"Where do you think you're going?"

"Anywhere. Wherever you're going." Again, she tried to appear fragile, in need of protection.

He scowled.

Holding his gaze with her own, she eased down to her knees.

His eyes changed from a purple-ish brown to a light violet and the sexy horns stiffened and leaned in her direction.

"I don't have any steins to pay you, but I promise I'll make it worth your while," she purred and worked the bulging form of his cock out of his tight black flight pants.

He swallowed, his large hand dropping to tangle in her hair. She watched him struggle for control. "How did you get on my ship?"

Was he really caressing her ear? An odd sensation moved in her—a small stirring of curiosity or excitement.

"I slipped in through the cargo. Please—" she tongued the sensitive place beneath the mushroom head of his cock, "let me stay. I won't cause you any trouble."

"Well, I guess a female of your talents—" he broke off and groaned as she swirled her tongue around the head of his enormous malehood, "—might be of some use on this ship...*ugh*." He grasped the back of her head and shoved her over his length, causing her to gag and her eyes to water.

She'd given hundreds of deepthroat blowjobs or rough *vecks* over the years as a sex slave. She'd learned to simply detach and let her mind float away, to become nothing more than flesh, a body devoid of personality. But the pilot pulled back when she choked and brushed his thumb over the moisture leaking from the corner of her eye.

"Forgive me." He rubbed her tears between his finger and thumb as if he found the substance fascinating. "I didn't mean to choke you. Your mouth is smaller than I'm used to."

She blinked up at him in surprise and he brushed her cheekbone with the backs of his fingers. "Try again, I won't choke you, beautiful."

She took just the head of his cock into her mouth, sucking hard.

His groan of pleasure kicked up her confidence—excitement, even, and she took him deeper, relaxing the back of her throat to swallow him down.

Though his thighs trembled and ball sac had grown rock hard, he didn't thrust again, but let her control the movement, his rough breathing sending thrills of excitement straight to her core. She'd never felt so powerful giving a male oral pleasure before. She'd never enjoyed seeing a male come undone. But this one...his guttural shout made her pussy clench, the way his huge hand cradled the back of her head to hold her in place—so gentle yet capable of snapping her neck with ease if he wanted to. She swallowed his seed as she'd been trained to do and licked him clean.

He gripped her nape and lifted her to her feet, as if she weighed nothing. "Blowjobs like that will certainly be accepted as trade." His gaze grew heavy-lidded. "But I do think you deserve punishment for stowing away on my ship." He rotated her to face away from him, then picked up her two hands and pressed them against the ship's wall. His exotic, masculine spice filled her nostrils. The heat of his torso radiated against her back and his breath feathered across her bare shoulder.

A surge of lust ran through her body, once more surprising her. What was it about this male that excited her, when no male had ever aroused her interest before? Her pulse sped as she waited to see what shape his punishment took.

He tugged up her short slave's gown. She wore the bare minimal underclothing, as required by her station—a tiny string threaded around her waist and through her buttocks to hold up a slip of spidersilk between her legs.

The pilot made an approving noise in his throat just before his huge palm clapped down on her ass.

She yelped, but didn't move from her position.

He rubbed away the sting. "Naughty slave girl, hiding on my ship." He slapped the other side. Unlike punishments she'd received at the hands of her masters, or at the training institute before, his purpose was obviously to arouse her, through the pain. She'd heard of such a thing, but never understood it.

Now, though, a sliver of interest flickered, her sex actually growing moist from his rough treatment. It didn't make sense. She'd been beaten on countless occasions, for a master's pleasure or as punishment, and it had never had this effect on her.

He continued the slow cycle of slapping and rubbing each side and she grew more and more agitated. How would that big purple cock feel inside her? Would he be rough or gentle? What positions did he like?

No. She needed to keep her head. Look for the opportunity to grab the laser gun.

He reached around the front of her hips and slipped his fingers under the gusset over her panties.

His middle finger traced up her slit to find her clitoris. She hid her surprise. He cared about her pleasure? Delaying his own?

He brushed a feather-light circle around it, so much less than she craved. A strange itchiness took over her body, sending tingles of heat across her skin and producing a darker, pulsing need in her core. He disappointed her by removing his fingers from her panties.

A sharp slap over her sex made her cry out.

"Have you been naughty, slave?"

A shout sounded from just beyond the door. She whirled and lunged for the laser gun on his holster, the element of surprise giving her the split second she needed to beat him to it.

With the barrel pressed against his chest, she lifted her chin toward the door. Nineteen escaped human slaves would've fanned out over the entire ship by now, taking the meager six-member crew hostage. She'd done her part and captured the toughest one.

"To the cockpit," she ordered. "We're commandeering your ship."

The rage on the purple-skinned being's face should have frightened her—and it did. But it also inspired a sliver of regret. She almost wished they'd had a chance to finish that act she normally detested so much.

Almost.

1

Rok glared at Lamira, the human female who looked just like the one who'd stolen his ship and left him stranded on the abandoned planet Pifany eight months ago. It had taken him and his crew three weeks and a lot of sweet-talking to find a lift back to civilization. Then it had taken another six weeks of the most dangerous smuggling work—piloting a borrowed ship into a war-torn planet of Jesel with weapons—to earn enough to buy a new airship.

In fact, he still hadn't recovered financially from the setback.

So to find a human who claimed to be Lily's sister peering from behind the so-called Zandian prince annoyed the *veck* out of him.

"Where is your *vecking* sister?"

Prince Zander drew himself up. "You will speak with respect to my mate."

Mate, huh? That gave him pause. The slip of a human was dressed in finery, but she wore a collar around her neck like a slave. Granted, the collar was embedded with enough Zandian crystal to buy him five new airships.

The crystal was the only reason he'd come to the Zandian prince's pod. His body required energetic recharge through crystal amplified sunlight, and Zandian crystal was impossible to come by anywhere else.

For one half-moment he considered picking up that little human—with the collar, of course—and making a break for it to his ship. He had no problem punishing one female for her sister's misdeeds and this one was certainly as pretty as Lily, although his body didn't have the magnetic attraction he'd experienced the moment he laid eyes on her. That's how the little witch had tricked him.

Too bad Zander had security guards everywhere and unlike him, they were around the crystals all the time, getting constant recharge. So while he had a lifetime of street fighting behind him, their strength probably outmatched his.

He met the darkened stare of the male who called himself prince. Prince of Nothing. Zandia had been occupied by the Finn for over twenty solar cycles.

The male glaring back did not look as weak or pampered as he'd imagined the royal nothing would be. In fact, he looked every inch the warrior—eyes alert with an assessing, intelligent gaze, hand on the hilt of a sword, not a laser gun.

He had to give grudging points for that. Maybe Zander wasn't just a pretty-boy living out his life on his country's remaining wealth.

Rok cleared his throat. "Forgive me, your highness." He didn't quite keep the mocking tone from his words.

The prince's eyes narrowed and then, before he had a chance to react, he found himself shoved up against the wall, the sheathed blade of the sword pressing down on his windpipe. "My mate asked you a question. How do you know Lily?"

He didn't fight back, knowing it would be useless in the prince's own pod with his guards everywhere. When Zander let up enough on the sword for him to speak, he croaked, "She stole my ship!"

The prince released him, surprise flitting over his features.

"So she *is* free!" Lily's sister bounced on her heels, looking excited. "Where? When?"

"Eight months ago, leaving Ocretia's capital. She and two dozen escaped slaves overtook my crew and forced us to land and deboard, so if you know where she is now, I'd really love to get my ship back."

Lamira licked her lips. The memory of her sister's lush mouth closing around his cock flashed through Rok's mind.

Yes, that was part of why he was so *vecking* mad. He'd known it was the oldest trick in the book and he'd still let Lily tempt him. His cock had taken the lead and he had lost everything he'd owned. What had it been about that pretty little human slave that had tempted him?

Mierna had said they had some sort of connection. What in the stars could it be?

"I've never met her, actually."

That surprised him.

"She was taken from our parents when she was just three, before I was born. I've spent my whole life hoping to meet her."

Zander extended his arm, fist raised at a ninety degree angle in the traditional Zandian greeting. "I am Zander."

Something painful tightened in his chest. He hadn't seen the gesture since he'd left Zandia, but he remembered its use. Remembered his father, a palace laborer, using it when he greeted other beings. He crooked his arm into the same shape and touched fists with Zander.

"Rok."

"Welcome to my pod, Rok. Please stay for the weekly meal so we can discuss Lily—" he glanced at Lamira, "and other matters further."

He arched a brow. What in the veck were the *other matters*? He really didn't have time to spare—his crew waited for him in the ship and they'd made the dangerous trip to Ocretia just for him to recharge.

"His crew," the human murmured.

Smart, for a human.

Zander's gaze flicked to her and back. "Your crew is also welcome."

He nodded once, slowly. "I'll go ask them, then. They may not want to stay." Mainly because he and three other of his crew members had warrants out for their arrest for smuggling in Ocretia.

"Prince Zander does not work for the Ocretian government," the human said.

A tingle washed over his skin. Did she read minds?

Zander shot her a warning look, but she laced her fingers in front of her, looking serene. "Many of us have reason to hide from them." She met his gaze squarely.

She certainly would, if she possessed mind reading powers. Humans with any aberrant traits were exterminated immediately. The ocretions bred their slaves for only one thing—servility.

Reason told him to get the *veck* out of there, fast. She knew about the warrants. It was probably a trap. She was Lily's sister, after all and that human had ruined the past eight months of his life. But his gut said to stay. Besides, curiosity nipped at his heels.

He wanted to know what this quirky human was doing with the prince of his species, and what they wanted from him. Because he sure as stars knew they both wanted something.

~.~

Lily dodged the flying debris from the firebombs, a sob stuttering in her too-dry throat.

Dead. The entire enclave of escaped slaves had just been found and demolished. If she hadn't been out foraging for food, she'd be dead, too.

Tears streaked her cheeks. They'd been like family to her. For the past eight months, she'd been free. Yes, it had been hard. Hiding out on the planet of Jesel, they'd hoped to emulated those humans who had fought for freedom there and won over four hundred years ago.

But Jesel had been in the midst of another war and had fallen to the Republicans once again. And funny, but the Republicans hadn't cared that she and her fellow escaped slaves weren't from Jesel. They were killing every human they could find.

She needed to get the veck off this planet, and fast. The trouble was, she had no one in the universe. No one to message, nowhere to go that would be safe for an escaped human slave.

Stumbling through the smoke, coughing the polluted air, she scrambled down into a crevice, where she could at least breathe. Her eyes stung from the smoke and ash and her knees, elbows and chin were bloody from when she'd been knocked on her belly by the blast.

A shallow river sliced through the canyon and she waded right into it, dropping to her knees, cupping the water in her hands and splashing the ash from her face. She screamed when a dark serpent shot out of the reeds and bit her ankle.

Vecking hell. She wished she'd died with the others.

She wouldn't survive out here alone. There were too many wild animals and natural dangers, even if she didn't have to worry about being hunted down and killed by the Republicans. She'd probably be better off using her laser gun on herself to save the terror and suffering of starving to death or being killed.

Veck that.

Her self-preservation instincts kicked in. She was a survivor. She'd somehow kept her soul after all these years in captivity, and now she was sure as veck going to keep it now that she'd found freedom. If she had to learn to live alone in the caves cut into these canyon walls, she would.

She heard a whistle to the left of her—a decidedly human whistle —and then an arrow whizzed by her head and hit the rock beside her. She grabbed the arrow and started running before she'd even figured out from which direction it had come.

In another moment, she was on the ground, pinned down by a large human male. "I got her," he cried triumphantly in the ancient language once used on Earth. "Wait till you see her—she's about as tasty as they come."

A fraction of her fear eased. If they were interested in using her body, she'd convince them to let her live. This was one situation—perhaps the only one—she knew how to handle.

~.~

Rok had never eaten so well in his life. The food served at Zander's table had been exquisite. They dined in his Great Hall, a magnificent room in his palatial pod. The walls were brightly colored, and crystals magnified the sunlight in here, too. Most fascinating, though, was the plethora of potted plants that made the room appear like a lush jungle. Food-bearing plants, from the looks of them.

An exiled prince lives a far different existence than the escaped laborer's son. A large group of Zandians had gathered for the meal along a long row of tables. Almost all were male, save a few elderly females, which explained why the prince had taken an alien mate. Still, his choice of a human suprised Rok. Although Lamira was admittedly special.

Not that he was prejudiced, either. He'd grown up among aliens of all kinds. He didn't have the luxury of presuming his species was better than another. But Zander and his pod were known for keeping to themselves, allowing only Zandians to work there or even enter the pod. The fact that Zander had invited his crew in for the meal meant he must really want something from Rok.

His crew sat at the far end of the table, but they didn't seem to mind being relegated to the lower class section. Janu and Jaso, his two foster brothers, kept raising their glasses toward Rok and Zander in appreciation of the delicious meal. He was grateful they'd shown some modicum of manners, as the small but ferocious Stornigians could be as rowdy as animals, especially when there was wine involved.

Mierna, his Venusian co-pilot, had also obviously indulged in the wine, but then she functioned half-drunk on a regular basis, so that was nothing new. His giant, one-legged friend Gaurdo, an Elau, ate heartily but watched the entire affair in wary silence. Rok had rescued him from a pack of wild beasts outside a trading station once. That was how he'd lost the leg.

Depri had also taken in everything, particularly the opulence of the palatial pod. He'd probably already devised a hundred schemes for how Rok and his crew could benefit from trading with Zander.

When the meal ended, Prince Zander, his human mate and her mother remained, along with four older males. Lamira was as beautiful as he remembered Lily, but without the fire behind her eyes. Lily had been magnificent—her treachery as impressive as the way she'd handled a weapon, the burning determination in her gold-flecked green eyes. And her scent...he still remembered that feminine musk. He'd stroked himself off to fantasies with her in the months since she stole his ship. Particularly to the thought of punishing her soundly for her misdeeds.

Lamira and her mother had grilled him on everything he knew about Lily, which was little. Their excitement at hearing about her was not diminished by what he considered the considerable unlikelihood she was still alive. Escaped slaves didn't last long in this universe or any other, for that matter.

Still, he had a feeling there was something else Zander wanted from him, so he wasn't surprised when at last, the prince asked if he and his advisors might have a word in private.

Lamira and her mother, Leora, stood. "Your destiny is woven with ours," she murmured, as if only half intending him to hear. "And it is great. You were born to lead armies."

Zander seemed to take this prediction in a stride, as if his mate normally spoke in riddles like a Venusian. Rok frowned, but didn't have time to respond, as Lamira had already glided from the room, one hand on a slightly swollen belly, signalling what he'd missed before—she was pregnant.

His crew waited for his command. He gave a single nod, which they would understand to mean, *retire to the ship but remain alert.*

When they had all left, Zander touched his fingertips together and leaned back in his chair.

"Your primary occupation is as a pilot?"

He narrowed his eyes. If this was coming back to the smuggling warrant, he needed to leave.

"Any battle experience?"

"Why? You planning on taking Zandia back?" he snorted.

The prince didn't answer.

He sat forward in his chair, interest spiking. "You *are,* aren't you?"

Zandians didn't lie. Well, *he* might lie, to get himself out of a pinch with officials, but true Zandians didn't. He watched Zander closely, waiting to see what he said.

The prince chose not to answer, which to Rok, was as good as confirmation.

He tried to remember the vow his father used to give and lifted his fist, elbow bent at ninety degrees. "On Zandian honor, I will not speak of anything I hear here."

Zander and the four warriors all held their fists aloft to acknowledge his vow.

"You have a battleship?"

"I may have access to a number of battleships."

Rok's eyebrows shot up. "Is that so? And you need pilots to fly them?"

"We are all experienced and battle-ready pilots," he said, indicating the males present. "But I need hundreds more. There aren't enough Zandians alive to build such an army."

"Do you have the coin to hire such an army?" It was a rhetorical question, really. The Zandian prince was known for his enormous wealth, gained not only from what he'd escaped with, but from years of savvy investments.

Zander nodded.

He considered. Stornigians trained in combat flight were easy to come by, but they'd be unlikely to engage and fight with another species. If he led them, however, they *might* be willing. Still, could he find hundreds? He could only think of a dozen he might ask.

"I may be able to round up an army. I'd be their commander, though."

Zander inclined his head. "How soon will you know?"

"How many do you need, exactly?"

"One hundred and fifty."

He pursed his lips. If he were a wise male, he'd tell Zander no, thank you, and leave as quickly as he could. The possibility of taking back Zandia seemed slim, even with battleships and financial resources. But Zandia was his home. It still danced in his dreams—the vivid colors, the honor of the species.

"It may take a few months," He hedged. "I have another job to do first." They didn't need to know it was another illegal weapons smuggling job.

Impatience flitted over Zander's face, but he nodded. "I'll be awaiting your reply." He stood and bowed.

Rok barely resisted rolling his eyes at the pomp, but the prince had earned a grudging respect from him. Far from sitting on his cushioned throne, it appeared the male had been amassing his fortune for a reason—he sought to regain his kingdom.

Rok had to appreciate that goal, whether he believed it attainable or not.

2

Lily dozed on hard ground, where she'd spent the past 48 hours being taken multiple times by each and every one of the eighteen human rebels. She hadn't resisted—she knew better than that. Instead, her mind had drifted off to her "safe place"—the one with rainbow-hued light beaming through crystals onto her skin, rejuvenating her, healing her. This was how she'd survived since the day she'd been placed into sexual servitude.

The humans who had taken turns on her had smaller cocks than Ocretions, so she hadn't torn or suffered physically. Not that she'd know if she had—numbness inhabited every limb.

The sound of an airship forced her onto her hands and knees and she staggered to her feet. One of the rebels grabbed her elbow and propelled her forward, toward the landing craft.

Every man in the camp ran forward, lifting weapons that didn't match the primitive lifestyle they led in the wild.

The door to the craft lifted and she blinked several times. *Could it be?*

No, she was delirious.

But the huge purple-skinned warrior who emerged *had* to be the same pilot whose ship they'd stolen when she escaped. How many horned purple-hued smugglers could there be?

His eyes swept over the group, and though his expression showed nothing, his gaze bounced over her twice—three times. Of course, it could be the fact that her clothing had been torn off so she stood naked in a crowd of clothed beings.

The smuggler addressed the men's leader, bringing out several cases of weapons. She couldn't hear any conversation, but it was obvious the rebels had expected the male and wanted the goods he brought.

He closed up the cases and stacked them on the ground outside the ship, then stood directly in front of them and folded his arms. This would be the negotiation stage.

The rebel leader said something.

The smuggler shook his head and answered back.

More head shaking and speaking. The smuggler lifted his chin in her direction and all the men turned.

The rebel holding her dragged her forward.

"No deal," the rebel leader said. "We've only had her for two planet rotations and there are no other human females alive on the planet. We need her to breed."

The smuggler appeared bored. "So pay the appointed price."

The rebel leader's brows slammed down. He bent his head together with one of his friends to consult in low voices.

"Fifty thousand."

"And the female."

He was negotiating to buy her? Her idiotic heart gave a leap of excitement, right before she remembered that the smuggler surely didn't intend to pick up where they left off. No, she'd stolen his ship and left him stranded on an uninhabited planet. He intended to exact revenge.

"We keep the female."

"Then the price is one hundred thousand." He had the bargaining face down pat, boredom sprawled over his features.

More downturned mouths and angry gestures. "Forty thousand and the female."

The smuggler considered. His purple gaze swiveled to her.

Unaccountably, her nipples stiffened, as if excited by his disinterested up-and-down sweep. She folded her arms across her chest, but not before the smuggler noticed, a momentary twitch at the corners of his lips making her humiliation complete.

"Forty-five. Bring me the female." He made an imperious gesture in her direction, no longer looking her way.

Her captor shoved her forward and she fell to her knees. As she crawled up to stand, her mind raced. Was she walking to her death? She figured there was at least a fifty percent chance of it.

Why, then, did hope keep fluttering in her chest?

She stumbled through the rebels and walked right up to the pilot. Though she ought to know better, she held her head high and met his gaze squarely with her best look of defiance.

She expected a face slap at best.

Instead, she found herself upended over his shoulder. His huge hand clapped down on her bare ass. The sting enlivened her, bringing awareness back to her abandoned body, sending prickles all across her flesh. Dearest Mother Earth did she really hope he wanted her for sex?

The pilot collected his money and carried her, still slung ignominiously over his broad muscled shoulder, up the ramp.

"What in the *veck* just happened out there?" a short, hairy humanoid—Stornigian if she knew her species right—demanded. "If you really just accepted a female in exchange for—" The male trailed off when the pilot dropped her to her feet. "*Her?* No vecking way. What are you going to do with her?"

The pilot's grin held menace. "Anything I want."

A shiver ran down her spine, but her pussy clenched. Why did this male always succeed in arousing her?

His huge hand dropped onto her nape and he steered her forward, into the ship. A door slid open revealing a tiny washroom with a toilet and shower. "Clean yourself," he growled. "I don't want to smell those *vecking* males on you."

Excuse the *veck* out of her. Like she could help it. She'd just been used as a *veck*-doll for forty eight hours straight.

"Jaso," he turned to face the Stornigian trailing them. "Stand guard at this door while I take off. The sooner we clear Jeselian airspace the better."

She was grateful when he shut the door on her, leaving her alone in the cramped quarters.

Washing off the residue of the sex and the men was a luxury she hadn't expected and she didn't plan to waste it. She flicked on a spray of water and stood beneath it, letting it soak her hair and sluice over her skin. The water felt hotter than she was used to, but she loved it, her muscles unknotting and releasing.

She closed her eyes, imagining the water cleansing not just her body, but her *vecking* soul. Like the rainbowed light of her imaginary safe place, it cleared away the muck, the foul experiences and beings she had contact with, leaving only her pure essence.

She paid special attention to the serpent-bite on her ankle. It had reddened over the past two planet rotations and now throbbed under the heat. *Veck*. She hoped her body could work out the poison on its own, because she doubted this ship carried antidotes or antibiotics and seeking care elsewhere would be akin to turning herself in.

The door banged open and she braced herself, expecting to see the small hairy Stornigian. Instead, the enormous pilot squeezed into the room.

Her nipples beaded at the sight of him, her mysterious attraction to this being heightened by the intimate proximity.

His irises appeared more violet than before and his horns stood as stiff as his cock, which bulged beneath his flight pants.

He stripped off his clothes without a word.

She hid her mild surprise. Fine. She knew how these scenes worked. "Couldn't wait, huh?"

His lips twisted into a sour expression. "Apparently not."

Her pulse quickened. His words implied he was there against his will—as if he couldn't stay away—and that idea thrilled some part of her. Especially because her body continued to respond to his nearness, heat flooding her core at the sight of his magnificent, muscled and scarred body.

He grabbed her around the waist, turning her at the same time, so she faced away from him, her ass pressed back against his muscular legs, his thick cock jabbing her lower back. "I believe you owe me this," he rumbled just before he shoved her up against the shower wall.

"Yes," she gasped.

"You agree?" He pulled her hips backward and pressed the head of his cock against her pussy.

"Yes."

"Good. Then we don't have to quarrel."

Unlike the eighteen males who'd just pummeled her sex, this one took care with her, rubbing his cock head over her entrance several times to test her readiness before easing in.

She gasped—his cock was far bigger than anything she'd taken before.

He froze, halfway in. "Take it," he growled, yet he didn't press further and his hand slid around the front of her hips, fingers questing for the button at the apex of her entrance.

He was the only male who had ever touched her there. She shrieked at the sensation, immediately pushing her hips back to take in the rest of him, then shuddering at the shock of it.

He stayed buried deep inside her, not moving. His fingers slapped her clitoris several times until she began to move her hips up and down, trying to gain more friction.

"Ready for me?"

Her internal walls contracted. *That voice.* Deep, masculine, powerful. Just like the cock he began to pump in and out of her.

"No," she gasped, though it wasn't from pain. It was all too much—the sensations of being filled by his huge length sent frissons of pleasure through her core and down her inner thighs.

He vecked her harder, faster.

"I'm sorry," she gasped. "For what it's worth. I'm sorry I stole your ship."

"You will be, Lily." The words were threatening, but the guttural tone promised sex.

She was surprised he remembered her name. But of course he'd probably been hunting for her.

"I plan to punish you in at least five hundred ways and when I'm through, I know someone who will pay a great deal for you. Maybe enough to even cover the cost of my ship."

If he hadn't been moving inside her, stroking her inner walls with his long cock in a way that made her eyes roll back in her head, she might have grown chilled by his promise to sell her. As it was, lights exploded behind her eyes as his enormous length rammed her inner walls and stretched her wide.

She noticed that while he had her mashed up against the wall, his own arms took the brunt of his force, protecting her from bruising her pelvis each time he shoved deeper. Like the other small considerations he'd shown, it added to her growing opinion that he might be a decent being.

Not nearly as cruel as he'd have her believe.

"Veck, Lily, you're so...*vecking*...tiny...so tight."

His pleasure and obvious loss of control gave her confidence, made her feel powerful—which was a first for her during sex.

He thrust upward with each word, lifting her off her feet, speared by his cock.

One of his huge palms closed over her left breast and he squeezed her nipple between his thumb and forefinger.

It was too much. Her body convulsed under his hold, pussy clenching and releasing around his enormous cock, shudders of shock and pleasure running down her legs, up through her torso.

Holy Earth. Holy Mother.

He withdrew and shoved deeper, deeper still, vecking her with a force she thought certain would crush her, and then he, too, found his finish. Hot streams of his seed filled her, leaking down her legs in a splash of pearlescent rainbow.

She stared at the substance, fascinated by the beautiful colors swirling down the drain.

He panted behind her, thankfully still holding her up, or she'd collapse on the metal floor.

"Did those humans hurt you?" His breath came hot against her ear, voice a deep rumble that went straight into her chest and reverberated.

The question surprised her. "No. I know better than to resist."

"Good. Did I?" He shut off the spray of water and warm air blew at them from all directions.

Did he what? *Oh.* For some unfathomable reason, her face grew warm. A sex slave felt no shame. Yet there she stood, blushing from a simple question.

Simple, yet complex.

"No." Her voice cracked. "It was no more than I can take."

He spun her around and shoved the wet hair from her eyes. "Good," he grunted. "Because I plan on putting my cock in every hole of yours daily until you beg for mercy."

He must be very foolish if he thought threatening her with sex would frighten her.

"Between beatings, that is."

Her breath halted.

His hand had dropped to cup her mons, though, middle finger gliding over her slit, spiking her temperature again, confirming her suspicion that this was all a game to him. He didn't harbor deep resentment, he was enjoying himself.

Stars, how did this male elicit such reactions from her?

She licked her dry lips.

He stared down at her mouth, as if disconcerted to see her tongue. "I'm looking forward to punishing you, Lily."

There. She'd known it.

"Let's get your first whipping taken care of. That way you can sleep it off and we can start again in the morning."

Truthfully, it didn't frighten her. She'd been punished in far worse ways than whipping as a slave, and she'd already begun to trust him enough to believe he wouldn't go too far. In fact, she almost looked forward to submitting to his punishment without a fuss. Would he find her unable to resist again?

Her gaze tangled in his amethyst one and her breath hitched as all thoughts rushed out of her brain. She became nothing but naked, trembling flesh, a blank canvas for him to paint upon. "I—I don't know what to call you."

"Rok."

She dropped her eyes and dipped a curtsy. "Master Rok," she murmured submissively.

His posture went rigid. He cupped her chin and lifted it. "Just Rok." His eyes had returned to dark brown. "I'm not your master, I'm a male exacting punishment in the way he likes best."

A shiver ran down her spine at the note of sadism. He made everything sound sexual. She remembered the spanking he'd given her the first time they'd met. Measured pain made to arouse. Yes, this male enjoyed blurring the lines between pain and pleasure. Strangely, that ignited far more excitement than fear.

"What species are you?"

Already dry, Rok pulled on his clothes. "Zandian."

She'd never heard of it.

He bent both her wrists behind her back and pinned them there with one hand. With a push of a button, the door slid open and he maneuvered her, completely naked, out through his ship.

A good slave would drop her eyes and walk humbly past the crew. But she didn't think it necessary to pretend. Something about the Zandian made her think he didn't care about those things. The game he played was his own, and she'd have to learn the rules.

She lifted her chin and stared haughtily back at the crew as they passed. Two Stornigians, the old Venusian she'd seen last time, an Elau and the thin one—a species she didn't know. They all gaped as she padded past in bare feet. He shoved open the door to a tiny sleeping compartment.

~.~

WHAT IN THE stars was he doing? Rok hadn't meant to barge into the washroom and *veck* the little human against the aluminum wall.

He'd seen the dead in her eyes back there on Jesel. He'd wanted to kill those *vecking* human men. She'd been ill-used. Enough that half her soul had fallen away, by the looks of it. But then he'd returned to relieve Jaso of standing guard and the thought of her, just beyond the door, naked save for droplets of water gliding over her skin, made him mad with desire.

The same thing had happened on their first meeting. He'd known she was playing him, offering to suck his cock to keep him from sounding the alarm that she'd escaped. He'd been ready to wrap a fist in her thick copper hair and tell her to smarten up. That he couldn't be so easily manipulated. That he might not return her to her owner, but she'd sure as *veck* have to barter something to keep him from turning her in.

Except he'd caught her scent. Watched those full lips part. Drowned in the depths of moss green eyes. And then he just had to let her barter the skill she had obviously perfected.

And it had cost him his ship.

Yes, he certainly planned to thoroughly punish the little human for the trouble she'd caused, and he'd let her think he planned to turn her into the Ocretions, because she deserved a little stress. But she had family yearning to see her. A younger sister who spoke like a Venusian and a wistful mother, still beautiful despite what had obviously been a hard life.

Her sister's beauty had not affected him like this. What was it about Lily that made her impossible to resist?

He guided her to his sleeping platform and pressed a hand between her shoulder blades, forcing her to fold at the waist and present her delectable little ass to him. It was skinnier than he'd like to see it. Perhaps on their twenty-six planet rotation journey to Ocretia she would add a little roundness to her elegant curves.

He wound a leather band around her wrists, tying a knot so could not escape. He slapped a second leather band against his palm, measuring its sting.

Not horrible. He slapped it against his leg. Yes, it would do.

"I'm going to whip you, Lily." He thought it only fair he explain what her punishment would entail. "It will be a hard punishment. You stole my ship and left me and my crew stranded for weeks on an abandoned planet."

In her vulnerable position, folded naked over his bed, hands bound, she appeared pale and penitent. But he wasn't fooled.

"This won't be your last punishment for your crimes. I intend to exact revenge in a variety of ways during our trip to Ocretia." He ran his large palm over her lovely ass, drawing a measured breath to still the surge of lust touching her incited.

The muscles in her back bunched up at that. Yes, he'd let her believe he planned to turn her in. She should be worried for her life. He stroked up her back, soothing her before he caused her pain. He liked her nervous, not terrified.

He brought the leather strap down across her buttocks, holding her wrists to contain her lurch of pain.

She cried out, then ducked her face into the bedcovers.

"This punishment," he brought the strap down again, making a second puffy red line below the first one, "will probably be the most severe, unless you anger me again on the trip."

Her muffled cry sounded from the covers.

He held her hip and applied the strap, whipping her over and over again. He liked hurting females, especially if they enjoyed it, but this time he didn't intend to play. He'd whip her thoroughly and get the rancour out of his system. A true punishment for a real crime. After that, he'd let himself enjoy having her at his mercy. That had been his initial plan, anyway. Of course, he'd already diverged from that course and *vecked* her, not waiting more than two minutes after he'd cleared Jeselian airspace and set the controls on autopilot.

Well, this should set things straight between them.

He snapped the thick leather strap across her lower buttocks.

She screamed.

He leathered her shapely ass from the top of the crack down to her thighs and back up again.

She didn't beg or plead, but she did make plenty of noise, yelping each time the strap slapped her flesh.

He whipped her, watching her pale skin turn a deep shade of red, then continuing for another ten strokes.

By the time he finished, her back shook with sobs. He steeled himself against the pang the sound produced in his chest.

He worked the knot on her bonds and freed her hands. Her little fists curled under her body, face still pressed in the bedcovers. He sat beside her and ran his hand over her slender back, admiring the delicate lines of muscle, her narrow waist, and of course, her beautiful welted ass.

"That's over with. Now, we can move forward."

Her back continued to heave with ragged breath.

He slid his fingertips into her thick hair and massaged the back of her head, her neck, one shoulder.

She turned her face to look at him, and he was surprised to find her eyes dry and a questioning expression on her face.

He stroked her flushed cheek with his thumb. "It's over now, pet."

Her breath slowly quieted. She still lay folded over the edge of the bed, rosy red ass on display.

His cock stirred. He wanted her again. But he wouldn't take her. She needed a good meal and some rest. Tomorrow he could whip her again, if he liked. Take it slow and show her how pain could bring pleasure when applied just right.

He stood up. "I'll get you some food. Crawl up in the bed. Don't move from it, or I'll punish you again when I return, and I'll make that last beating seem like a caress. Understand?"

She immediately obeyed, crawling up to flop on her belly on the bed.

He gripped one ass cheek, thumb nested down against her anus and gave it a possessive shake. "Answer me, pet."

"Yes, master—I mean, Rok."

"Good girl." Satisfaction at her easy obedience made his chest hum. She didn't seem resentful over her punishment, which came as a relief.

He slipped out and locked the door from the outside, setting the controls so only his handprint opened the door from either side. Almost immediately, his body rebelled at being apart from her. He wanted to keep her close, as if her body provided some energy he required just to live.

Jaso and Janu were in the kitchen, preparing a basic meal of grain, dried fruit and erk bird meat. Both his foster brothers narrowed their eyes and watched him with an accusing stare as he walked in and dished a helping into a bowl.

He didn't require food as often as most species—only once every dozen planet rotations, as long as he stopped at Zander's pod for a crystal recharge at least once a month. Growing up on Stornig without the crystals, he'd had to eat more frequently, and even then had been weak and unhealthy. He hated that he needed to recharge with something he didn't control, although Zander never charged his species for their use, and made his palace open once a week to those who needed it.

"I seriously hope you have a plan for recuperating the steins you just lost us in taking that ship-stealing piece of human filth," Janu said.

"You're going to turn her in for the warrant money or sell her to the Zandian prince so he has a twin set, right?" Jaso challenged.

His lip curled, annoyance flashing through him. He may very well have been planning to bring her to Zander, requesting, of course, compensation for the loss he took in "rescuing" her. But his brother's insinuation that Lily would become Zander's second sex slave bothered the piss out of him. So did the reference to her as human filth.

He didn't know much about humans, but they seemed to be of

great use to the Ocretions, and this particular one was not unpleasant to look at it. To say the least.

"Yes," Janu jumped in, "please tell us this isn't about getting your big purple cock sucked by a pretty little mouth, because we could've bought you a human slave a year ago and saved all of us a world of trouble."

He scowled, tempted to stalk away without giving either one of them an answer.

But that wasn't fair. They had suffered as much as he had as a result of Lily's deception. Of course, it wasn't all her—there had been close to two dozen other stowaways who helped her take the ship.

"I plan to punish her, which you know I shall enjoy, and then yes, collect a ransom on her, either from Prince Zander or the Ocretion slave enforcement."

A smirk formed on Jaso's lips, appeased now that Rok had admitted to his fetish.

"I'm not thinking entirely with my *giant* purple cock."

Janu tossed a cleaning cloth at his face. He ducked and let it fly over his back.

"You sharing her?"

That same current of irritation ran through him. "*No,*" he growled. Then, realizing he'd spoken too sharply, tried to make it light. "I thought you considered her a filth, anyway."

Now Janu smirked, too. "Beautiful filth. That Zander knew what he was doing when he bought her sister."

His teeth clenched. "Right."

Discussing Lily and her sister had become no less annoying to him, so he picked up the food and left the twins to their own meal.

In his chamber, Lily appeared to have obeyed, still lying in the position he left her. The sight made something high in his chest squeeze. A fierce, protective urge rose in him. This fragile human, this delicate, lovely female's safety lay in his hands now. He would make sure to keep her safe.

She lifted her head, eyes on the food and a pang for not feeding her first ran through him. She hadn't eaten for several planet rotations, judging from the attention she paid the bowl. She eased up to kneel, wincing when her ass hit her heels, then choosing instead to stand on her knees.

The sight nearly undid him.

She looked every inch the sex slave—pert breasts offered up, her sex—permanently made bare through laser hair removal, as was the custom with Ocretion sex slaves—gloriously inviting between her legs, copper hair tumbling across one shoulder. If some being told him that she was actually a mystical, magical creature, capable of seducing males of every species and bringing them to their knees, he would've believed him. Her sister had possessed some extra-human ability to read minds, why couldn't this one possess some quality that made her irresistible to him?

He stepped closer and she reached for the bowl, but he pulled it back, out of range. "Uh uh. I'll feed you or you'll eat too fast. How long has it been since you've fed?" He scooped up a spoonful of grain and fruit and held it out to her.

Her lips closed around the utensil immediately and she answered with a full mouth, "Since they captured me, two planet rotations ago."

"You were only with them two planet rotations? That's good." Though he shouldn't care, the idea of her being mistreated by those men made him uncomfortable.

She watched the spoon expectantly, but he paused, not wanting her to make herself sick by eating too quickly.

"It was time enough for each one of them to take me several times each."

The bitterness in her tone ripped his chest open. He'd half convinced himself that as a sex slave, she'd known no better—apart from her brief freedom when she'd stolen his ship. He hadn't wanted to pity her for her station in life. Because if he did, it would make everything he'd done to her wrong, as well.

Veck.

"I'm sorry."

Her eyes shifted from the bowl to his face, surprise flickering there.

He swallowed and picked out a piece of meat. "Chew it slowly," he warned. "How often to humans normally feed?"

She chewed frantically and swallowed. He rolled his eyes.

"Three times a day, if we can. Sex slaves are generally well-kept. They want us looking healthy, of course. But we'd been foraging on Jesel for half a solar cycle, so we didn't eat as often as we liked."

"You and who? The rebels?"

She shook her head and made an impatient jerk of her chin toward the bowl. He smiled. She was adorable. He loved when she showed him this real side of her, what lay beneath the slavish meekness. Lily, the warrior. The one who'd stolen his ship. He fed her another bite.

"The escaped slaves. The ones who took your ship."

"Hold on," he barked. "Is my old ship back there on Jesel?" He would turn around and recover the thing, if it was.

"It didn't survive landing."

He growled his displeasure.

She shrugged. "They'd only learned to fly by scanning databases. No one had any practical experience, so we figured we were lucky to walk away from the landing."

He swore several times and walked a tight circle around his small chamber.

She climbed down from the bed and followed him, attempting to take the bowl from him with adorable supplicant eyes.

Once more, he jerked it back, but offered her a bite. Her little tongue darted out to catch a spilled piece of grain on her lip and he watched it, fascinated.

He really shouldn't be so turned on by this silly human.

"So what happened to the rest of them? The escaped slaves?" He wasn't sure why he wanted to know, but he did. He wanted to hear all of her stories, too—how they'd planned the escape, what her life had been like. But that was just bizarre.

Her pretty face clouded and her muscles hardened. "They were killed," she said stiffly.

"By whom? The rebels?"

"No. By a bomb. I was away from camp." Her gaze turned distant, like she was reliving the moment.

He didn't want her to.

"Again, I'm sorry."

The long dark lashes lifted and she studied his face, as if checking for sincerity. "I don't understand you," she muttered.

He fed her another bite of food and handed over a bladder of juice with a tube attached. She bit the end off and drank the entire thing down.

He lifted his chin. "Get on the sleeping platform. I think you've had enough food for now."

She opened her mouth as if to protest, but he shook his head. "I promise I won't let you go hungry."

~.~

LILY WHIMPERED *as the rebel slapped her face and pushed her backward, forcing her to the ground. Her wrists were tied together and he held the end of the rope, which he jerked above her head, until she lay flat. "Spread your legs, slave, you don't get to walk around our camp."*

His force came down on her too hard and he stank of the worst body odor she'd ever smelled. Her former masters had at least been clean and kept her in comfortable surroundings. They'd been upper class, so they possessed the wealth to own their own pods and have steady access to food.

He came down on her, ready to shove his cock in her mouth.

"No," she moaned and turned her head to the side.

"Hush, Lily, it's a dream.."

Confusion twisted through her consciousness as she tried to match the voice to the filthy human holding her down.

Her body jerked and she blinked up at a horned alien warrior. *Rok.*

Her wrists were still bound together with the other end of the rope attached to Rok's wrist, the way he had secured her before they fell asleep.

Holy one true sun, he was beautiful. His hairless jaw was square and strong, hair sandy brown around the stiffening horns. His eyes glowed with violet rimmed irises. He leaned against the wall behind his bed with his magnificent chest bare.

His eyes traveled from her face down to her bare breasts and grew more violet, hunger evident in his gaze. She was accustomed to being ogled in every way, had learned to use a male's interest to guide or distract him into some form of sex act that might be the least invasive at the moment.

Never before had a lustful gaze made her body heat in response.

Her nipples beaded, breasts grew taut.

"You're finally awake. I've been waiting to torture you for hours."

She wasn't sure how to take that statement. It produced a shiver, and the memory of the past night's whipping returned to her in full force. Yet a tinge of excitement coated everything as well.

He unwound the leather strip that bound his wrist first, then the one around the two of hers. His examination of the red marks, and the way he rubbed his thumb over them as if trying to erase them made something flutter in her belly.

Did she hope he cared? She considered showing him the serpent bite on her ankle. It had continued to fester, the throbbing a dull background pain to everything. But she didn't want him to take her somewhere for medical care, because it would mean her immediate arrest. No, better to wait it out. Hopefully she would recover on her own.

Looking to Rok to save her was stupid. She was his captive and he was bent on enacting punishment in a way he clearly enjoyed. When he was through with her, he planned to collect the warrant on her, which meant her certain death.

So basically, she needed to find a way to escape or she'd be dead when they reached Ocretia.

Rok tugged her torso over his thighs so she lay face down, ass up. His large hand traced over her buttocks. "Is this normal for a human?" His voice choked with shock.

She twisted around to look. Her ass still wore the splotches from his whipping—patches of red standing out brightly on her normally pale skin.

Did he regret it?

If so, she wasn't going to tell him that it no longer hurt and probably wouldn't unless he picked up his strap and used it again. She opted for a sulk, instead. "You whipped me—*hard*." That was not a lie.

"How long does it take you to heal?" He still sounded choked.

"I don't know, seven to ten planet rotation, probably."

Rok abruptly lifted her from the spanking position and plopped her beside him. Some of the color had drained from his face. "Well," he said stiffly, "Humans are more fragile than I knew. Not good for punishing at all."

She hid her amusement. "Most find us extremely good for punishing. The pain of a lesson lasts for a long time."

His lip curled. "I suppose if you're training a slave, that's useful." He sounded disdainful.

Perhaps she'd taken it too far. He enjoyed delivering punishment and now believed she was unfit for it. She didn't want him to lock her away until he collected the warrant. She'd have a far better chance of escape if she remained in his chamber as his slave. And she didn't care to examine that other, small part that *might* enjoy being near him. Even craved his attention and his touch.

She rose up on her knees and reached for one of his horns. She'd seen how they stiffened and leaned just like his cock during arousal. They must be a sensual part of his anatomy.

He shuddered when she fisted it, allowing her to tilt his head down.

She pressed her breasts in his face and swirled her tongue around the horn.

Rok's breath turned ragged. He palmed one breast, squeezing harder when she took the entire horn into her mouth. Though as short as her thumb, it was the same girth as a human cock, and it stiffened and grew as she sucked it. His lips closed on her other nipple, tongue flicking it.

Rok looped an arm around her waist, pulling her closer as the fingers of his other hand slid between her thighs.

Surprise flitted through her when she realized how wet he'd found her pussy—it practically dripped, her folds swollen and slick. He screwed one, then two digits inside her, making her gasp with pleasure.

"Suck harder," he grunted and plunged his fingers in and out of her, filling and stretching her.

She obeyed, hollowing her cheeks and sucking as hard she knew how, bobbing her head up and down over his horn.

Rok found the bundle ofnerves on her inner wall and her inner thighs trembled. She moaned over the horn. One finger of his other hand sought her anus.

She stiffened.

"Keep sucking." His voice sounded low and gravelly.

She whimpered, but obeyed, both wanting and not wanting him to continue working her with his fingers. It seemed she had no choice- he finger*veck*ed her pussy as he worked one digit into her back hole and *veck*ed her there, too. Her insides fluttered. Heat flooded her pelvis.

He shouted a curse and she realized he was coming. He withdrew his fingers from her and shoved his sleeping pants down to fist his cock.

"No, don't stop," he gasped when she adjusted her mouth. In two pumps, he arrived, ribbons of rainbow-hued seed spurting like a fountain from the slit of his cock.

She continued sucking his horn until he finished and his eyes went heavy-lidded.

He grasped her waist, tossing her to her back and climbing over the top. "Good slave," he purred. "Very "good girl. How did you know about the horns?"

She attempted a shrug, which was impeded by his weight, pressing her down onto the sleeping platform. "I guessed."

"Clever female. "You've been trained very well, haven't you?" His cock, though he'd just orgasmed, prodded her entrance.

She rocked her hips up to meet it, desperate for her own release after the incredible fingering.

"If I weren't still angry with you for stealing my ship, I would let you have my cock right now. I can see how much you need it."

She frowned at his arrogance and turned her head sharply to the side.

He chuckled. "Don't think you can hide it, little female. You're going to be on edge until I allow you to orgasm. Since I can't punish that pretty little ass of yours, I'll have to torture you this way." To her shock, he bent down and took her nipple between his lips, sucking and nipping at it until both her breasts ached and her pussy wound tight with need. "There will be no touching on your part. If you touch yourself, I will whip you again, sore ass or no. The only way you're going to get satisfaction is when I decide you deserve it, understand?"

She blinked at him. This was not a game she'd ever played. On the surface, it sounded deceptively easy. All she had to do was not touch herself or orgasm? Fine. She never did either of those things.

Yet he had inspired a restlessness in her, an itchy desire that, for the first time, she needed to scratch with something bordering desperation.

He pushed the tip of his cock inside her and she relaxed. He'd just been teasing. It was some form of joke. But then he withdrew it again, watching her face closely.

Damn him! She certainly showed her frustration when he pulled out.

He repeated the torture once, twice. On the third time, she turned her head to the side, determined to float away, as she'd learned to do during sex, but he caught her jaw.

"Look at me," he growled. "You want my cock?"

She thrust her jaw forward, not wanting to answer.

He shoved in all the way this time, his cock stretching her wide, stroking her inner wall. "Answer me, Lily." He pulled all the way out.

She gave a sob of frustration. "Yes! Okay? I want your cock. Are you happy, you arrogant—"

He covered her mouth his his large hand.

It was a sign of her growing comfort with this being that she dared call him names. Even so, she wouldn't have been surprised if he'd slapped her at the least.

He cut off her breath with that hand over her mouth, plunged in again, rocked his hips to scythe in and out three, four times, then released her, pulling out and climbing off the sleeping platform, his back to her.

She gasped, her pussy clenching around emptiness, her lungs filling and releasing without satisfaction. She'd been so. Close.

Rok's sleeping pants hung low in back, showing the top of his muscular ass. His broad shoulders stretched a mile, built of solid muscle and scars, large and small, covered his skin. Something about those scars made him all the more appealing to her. They proved him to be the rugged warrior he looked like. Or maybe it was because he'd known as much hardship as she had.

"I supposed you're hungry again?"

"Yes, master."

He turned around with a frown. He didn't like that title for some reason, but she didn't understand why not. There were so many things she didn't understand about him. Like how he could enjoy hurting females and act so caring at once? There was something so darkly treacherous, so seductive about him.

She feared, more than any threat facing her welfare, she would grow attached to him. To his attention, his consideration. The way he'd fed her, watching to make sure she didn't overeat, his reluctance to continue punishing her when she still showed marks, to the way his eyes turned dark purple when he wanted her.

He rummaged in a cabinet. "There aren't any flight suits that will fit you, but you can wear my undershirt." He tossed her a thin synthetic shirt in white.

She pulled it over her head.

Rok's eyes travelled to her breasts, and his lids drooped.

She glanced down. Though the shirt was huge on her, falling to mid-thigh, the thin material made it hug her breasts, her steepled nipples poking through.

Rok pinched one nipple through the shirt and the silky fabric slid over it, sending a shiver straight to her core.

She glared up at him and crossed her hands over her chest, not wanting to show how hot and bothered he had her.

He picked up her hand. "I don't need to tie you up, do I, Lily?"

She loved when he called her by her name. Some masters had, but most called her "slave." Even those who had used Lily, always made it sound disapproving, like her name was a bad word. In Rok's deep rumble, though, it somehow sounded sensual or even like an endearment.

But that was crazy. She was definitely reading too much into this male. He was a species she hadn't encountered before and she wasn't used to his ways, that was all. Soon she'd learn how to get by and come up with a plan to free herself.

"Do I?" He arched a stern brow.

"No, master Rok."

HIs lip curled at her use of the title master again, but he didn't say anything. Her hand fit in his palm like a child's in the larger one of a parent. There was both comfort and safety in the gesture.

A memory of her tiny hand encased in a man's flitted in her mind. Her father, perhaps? Before she went to the institute to be trained as a slave? It must be, because she had no memories of anyone ever holding hands at the institute. All they knew there was complete subservience and swift and painful correction when they protested.

She couldn't remember a mother, specifically, but she knew she'd had one. She didn't remember a face or an incident, but she seemed to recall a feeling of love and safety. The energy of a mother. Some larger force that cared for her in a sweet and tender way.

Did Rok embody some essence of that? Was that what disturbed her so much about him?

She shook off the thoughts. They would not help her survive this. She needed to concentrate on a plan. She had to get free.

~.~

Torturing Lily by withholding her orgasm also tortured him. At least he'd taken the edge off when she'd sucked his horn. Holy Zandian star—he'd never had a female do such a thing—hadn't even known what it would do to him. Yes, he liked to rub his own horns, and he particularly liked to run them over the flesh of a willing female, but when she'd sucked it into her hot little mouth, he'd been in pure ecstasy. Yes, he planned to make her perform that task at least twice a day until they reached Ocretia.

He looked down at the beautiful little waif padding barefooted beside him.

"You're more agreeable than I'd expected," he observed.

She tilted her face up to his, her sensual lips curving into a wry grin. With her free hand, she touched the barcode at the back of her neck. "I'm a slave, aren't I?"

"Yes, but you're not particularly subservient, either." He stopped and pushed her up again the wall, trapping her there to show his far greater strength.

She tilted her lovely face up to his, her green eyes flashing with spirit. He loved that he didn't find fear or resentment there. Excitement, yes. And curiosity. She liked being his prisoner, he was sure of it.

"I like the rebellion in you," he rumbled. He was so *vecking* hard for her again, her scent filling his nostrils, her soft coppery hair brushing his face. "I'm surprised it was never beaten out of you." The idea of some previous master punishing Lily both enraged and turned him on. He hated to think of any master abusing Lily, yet the idea of taking her to task himself kicked his lust into overdrive.

"I usually hide it better."

He *vecking* loved that answer. He heard flirtation in her voice, as if she fully understood his game and wanted to play. "Do you think I should act more slave-like to my new master?"

She knew he didn't like her calling him that—he could tell by the wicked glint in her eye. Well, he preferred that feistiness to the docile show. He eased away from her and tugged her down the corridor.

He didn't want her to call him master. That was what Taraw had called him—Depri's sister, the female he had once loved. Besides, he didn't believe in keeping slaves. Zandians never had kept another species in slavery—he remembered his father being proud of that, even though it meant his father had to put in hard labor. "Other species would use slaves for physical labor, Rok," he would say, "But on Zandia, we aren't afraid to use our bodies to build things." His father had been proud of his station, low that it had been. "I built the palace the royal family lives in," he would say proudly. "I keep things running there. I'm part of a system that works without degrading other beings."

That was why it had bothered him so much to see the prince with a collar around his human mate.

They entered the kitchen and he pulled out a meal pack, unwrapped it and added water to reconstitute it.

Mierna drifted in, a tube of cheap grain alcohol in her hand. "Good," she said, jerking her head at Lily. "She belongs with you."

He rolled his eyes. Mierna always had predictions about his future—some great destiny he had to fulfill. Excrement, all of it. He didn't believe in destiny, and he sure as stars didn't see any higher purpose in his life. He'd been cobbling together an existence as a smuggler for the past ten solar cycles and the one thing he'd learned was to never make plans for a future, because excrement happened.

He learned to play things by the seat of his pants, taking every moment he remained alive as a win.

"You sure she belongs with me? Last time she put a laser gun to my chest and stole my ship."

The old Venusian nodded sagely. "There will be more trouble before it's done. Much more."

Despite his steadfast determination that fate did not exist in a universe of free will, her words made him tighten his lips. Would he have more trouble from Lily?

Probably so.

Her docile demeanor belied a quick-witted and devious character. One not unwilling to sacrifice others for her own gain.

He scowled at her, surprised when she shrank back from him. She was more sensitive to his thoughts that he'd expected. Another reason not to underestimate her.

Which didn't mean he wouldn't be sure to wring every bit of pleasure he could out of punishing her.

"Yes, have your fun," Mierna said, waving her hand as if to dismiss it all. "No harm in it. Both will enjoy."

He looked back at Lily and wondered if Mierna actually knew what he wanted to do to the human. He rather hoped not.

He handed Lily the paper tray with the reconstituted meal and watched her eat, wondering how else he might torture his little prisoner.

A wicked idea formed in his head. He searched the cabinets until he found the things he wanted—bree oil—a flavoring used by Depri for his food. It had a spicy, warming quality that would work perfectly. He also used a root vegetable as an aromatic spice. It, too, produced heat. Of course, the human was delicate. He'd have to watch her closely. But if it worked, it would be perfect for keeping her on edge.

She finished eating and deposited her waste in the incinerator, which immediately turned it to dust.

"Lift up your shirt."

"Isn't this your shirt?" she shot back, but her fingers reached for the hem.

"Did you get mouthy like that with your old masters, Lily?"

"No, master," she conceded.

"Good. Higher." He nudged the shirt above her peach-tipped nipples.

He uncorked the bottle of oil and dabbed a circle on each breast.

"Why good?"

"I'm glad you're willing to give me a little sass. It gives me reason to punish you."

Her face flushed an enchanting shade of pink. "Why do you like to punish?"

He dropped his hand to her pussy and rubbed the oil that remained on his fingers on her clitoris.

She clung to his arms, her legs wobbling as he stroked slowly over her slit.

"Because," he bent his head and murmured close to her ear, "it's so *vecking* hot to control all the responses of a female."

Her breath had quickened, fingers tightening until her nails dug into his skin.

"But why punishment?" She let out a sexy whimper and her eyes rolled back in her head.

He shoved her back against the wall and plunged his fingers deep inside her. "Because some little females deserve to be punished. Don't they?" He pumped them in and out.

"Oh!" Her face had flushed a deep pink and her fingers flew to her breasts. The oil had started working.

"Do you deserve my punishment, Lily?"

The involuntary twitch near her mouth made him yank his fingers out of her. She'd been about to orgasm.

She sobbed, her big eyes both pleading and accusing as she doubled over and reached one hand between her legs.

"Ah ah," he said sharply.

Her hand stopped just before it reached her sex.

"What did I tell you, pet?"

"No touching," she whispered. She took on a feverish appearance, eyes glassy, body shivering.

She cupped her breasts. "May I—"

He shook his head and she froze.

Her brows came down in frustration and she shoved at him, throwing her entire weight into his chest.

It was delicious. He loved the fight in her, He caught her up into his arms and held her off the ground while she kicked and scratched.

"Careful, pet. I don't want to have to spank you again, not until that pretty bottom heals."

"Oh the entertainment is in here," drawled Jaso from the doorway. Janu stood beside him, and they both wore smirks.

Lily instantly stopped fighting, dropping her chin and turning sullen, her face still flaming.

He tucked her against his side, protectively. He didn't mind a little humiliation, but any more would work against him and his plans to enjoy his lovely pet. Because truthfully, he needed her to enjoy his game, too, or else it wouldn't be fun for him. She might fight him, curse him, say she hated him, but as long as her sensuous body continued to show signs of arousal and excitement, he considered her to be playing along. He knew, though, if he took things too far—if he gave her more pain than she could handle or humiliated her too much, that part of her would shut down. He'd already seen glimpses of how she checked out of her body. And he definitely didn't want an empty *veck*-doll.

Not in the least.

"Come, pet. Let's not give them a show. You may either have some alone-time locked in my chamber or you may come to the exercise room with me."

"Exercise room," she said immediately.

Her answer pleased him, though he wasn't stupid enough to believe it was because she wanted to be near him. He needed her close, though. Liked to look on her pleasing form, to feel her closeness, smell her scent.

Yes, the little human pleased him a great deal. Far more than he'd expected, although he might have guessed based on his initial reaction to her the day she stole his ship.

~.~

LILY HAD NEVER BEEN HELD against a male's side while he walked. Even more intimate than the way he'd held her hand, it once more stirred her oldest memories. She'd been held. Picked up. She almost remembered the snippet of a song a female had sung to her.

To push back her panic at the swelling emotions within her, she searched for stable footing. "So how did you become a smuggler?"

He shrugged. "Scrappy trade for a scrappy male."

"And your crew? You seem close." She noticed he had the same crew as when she'd stolen the ship, despite the fact that they must have been grounded while he scrapped for a new craft.

"Jaso and Janu are my foster brothers. Their parents took me in after I escaped genocide on my planet."

She nearly stumbled, so surprised by this revelation. So his scars didn't lie—he had lived a rough life, like her.

"How old were you?"

"Eight solar cycles."

"How did you escape?"

They entered an exercise room. It had equipment along the walls but the center had been left as open space and contained only a floor mat.

"I got lucky. I lived in the palace because my father was a worker there. A guard scooped me up with two other children—daughters of an important advisor—and got us to an underground tunnel the moment the invasion started. He tried to go out and fight, but the tunnel was sealed from the palace end. We walked in the other direction for many kilometers and exited through a long-abandoned docking station. The guard boarded us on a ship and flew us out of there. I don't know how—it seems a miracle to me now." Rok rubbed his face. "Then he got shot down over Stornig and I was adopted by those dogs."

"What happened to the girls—I mean, the female young?"

His face clouded. "I never knew. I don't even know if they survived the crash."

Jaso and Janu filed in, along with the other three crew members. It seemed this was an appointed exercise time.

The wizened Venusian peered into her face. "Do you like to fight?"

"Wha—? Oh, no." She shook her head. She'd had docility trained into her at a young age with shocking forks. Any slave-child who showed aggression found herself immediately immobilized, pain shutting down her central nervous system.

"Me neither. Come—we'll exercise on the equipment."

She didn't know how to use the equipment, either, as exercise had also been forbidden, unless a slave required certain training by her master, but she followed the Venusian after shooting Rok an inquiring glance.

"What are you called?"

She bit her tongue to keep from muttering, "slave." Something about this crew made her far more at ease than she would normally be. "Lily."

"I am Mierna."

"Why haven't you introduced your prisoner properly, Rok?" one of his foster brothers taunted.

She enjoyed their playful banter and the way Rok ignored it. She hadn't been around such lighthearted ribbing before. Ocretions were always formal and stiff with the class system fully regimented. No one teased in the pods she'd lived.

Rok sighed and rubbed the back of his neck. "Come here, Lily." He beckoned her back to his side.

She dutifully returned, keeping her eyes lowered out of habit.

"Lily, you've already seen Jaso and Janu, my brothers. This is Gaurdo," he lifted his chin at a giant, rock-like being, almost as wide as he was tall. One of his legs had been amputated, and he had a metal post in its place. "And Depri." He indicated the tall, thin being with brown skin and green eyes. "He is also a brother, of sorts."

"Also from Stornig?" She wasn't sure what made her think it was appropriate to quiz them, but no one seemed troubled by it.

"No, we met them on one of our early expeditions." She wondered who "them" was, but something had clouded in Rok's expression so she no longer felt comfortable asking.

"How about you?" she asked Mierna as the old female steered her back toward the equipment. "How did you become a part of this crew?"

"They freed me from imprisonment in Bangi. I had nowhere else to go, so I joined them."

Her words sent such a streak of longing through Lily's chest she almost couldn't breathe. Her present situation was not unlike what Mierna described. This crew had helped her escape slavery—although not willingly—and she had nowhere in the galaxy to go. She did not have a single friend or family member. Nothing. To be invited in as a crewmate on this aircraft would be a fate beyond her dreams.

She thought back to the day she'd escaped. What would've happened if she hadn't stolen their ship? Rok had seemed content to accept payment for her fare in sexual trade. Would he have offered her a position when she told him she had nowhere to go?

She shook her head to clear the thoughts. She couldn't think this way. Her situation wasn't the same. She was wanted by the Ocretions—Rok couldn't keep her aboard a ship that traveled through the galaxy on dangerous trade missions. She'd threaten the safety of all of them. He'd be accused of transporting runaway slaves and put to death along with her.

The males had begun sparring in hand-combat in the center, one on one. Her eyes followed Rok's graceful movements. Though he was large, he moved with fluidity and ease, as if born fighting. The twins fought fast and dirty, lunging in, clamping sharp teeth on their opponent, but apparently not biting down.

Mierna handed her one end of an elastic band attached to the wall. She followed Mierna's action, pulling an elastic band out and in with her arm in different positions, mimicking it. Her muscles grew tired after only a few repetitions, but she kept at it. If she planned to escape and survive, she needed to become strong. These beings could show her how. Perhaps even teach her to fight.

The old Venusian nodded as if she knew Lily's thoughts. "Your destiny is much bigger than you see now. Do you know that?"

A tingle ran across her skin. She'd always had the sense that something came *after*. That sexual slavery wasn't her only episode in life. That belief had kept her from desperation or depression. Kept her from contemplating suicide, like some of the other girls.

But the Venusian might say such things to everyone. She hadn't said anything specific, and it probably didn't mean anything.

"I-I don't know," she murmured.

The old being nodded again. "You do know. You have always known. A great destiny. You will help many other beings find freedom and peace. Rok does not believe in destiny, yet he, too has one he must face."

Her doubt increased, even as the hairs on her arms stood up. For a few months there, she'd believed such a thing. She'd been a part of an escape plan and had learned to survive in the wilderness. She'd thought they might build a new human community of free beings.

But it had been too good to be true. Just when she'd started to care about something, it all had been destroyed. Every being she'd grown to love, every hope and dream crushed.

And now she was on a ship, rushing to her death.

"You will not die yet," the old Venusian said softly, turning away to repeat the exercises with her other arm.

Lily's breath caught.

The female did read thoughts.

3

Rok couldn't wait to get Lily back in his bedroom for her final torture. Keeping her on edge all day had been his own delicious deprivation, as well. He'd been hard for her all planet rotation. Stars, just having her in the exercise room while he sparred made his aggressive hormones flow to a height he'd never before experienced. He'd nearly harmed his brothers twice throwing them to the ground. In the end, they'd gone four-on-one instead of the usual two-on-one, because no one, not even Gaurdo, could hold him back.

They'd accused him of showing off for his slave.

Perhaps he had been. Her green eyes followed every move he made, though he sensed neither approval nor disapproval at his performance. All he knew was her mere presence in the room gave him the knife-like certainty of winning. He supposed it was a primitive response to enable a male to protect his mate.

Not that he considered Lily his mate.

He kept her close to him all day, pinching her nipples and rubbing between her legs every moment they were alone to keep her wet for him. Her scent filled his nostrils, inciting lust sharper than the crack of a whip.

Which, sadly, he wouldn't be using on her.

He didn't mind—what he had in store was far better.

He fingered the aromatic root he'd cut into perfect form and wrapped for her punishment. "Come, Lily." He picked up her hand.

She glanced up at him through her thick lashes, lips parted, the copper sheet of her hair falling over one shoulder. By the Zandian moons, she was lovely. So *vecking* lovely. Maybe he wouldn't return her to Zander. The prince didn't deserve two females this beautiful. He could make it part of his price for leading an army of airships on the Finn. One hundred thousand steins and your mate's sister as my...what? Slave? No, he'd been thinking *mate*.

Vecking excrement.

He ushered his slave into his chamber and locked the door. "Since your bottom is too tender for more punishment, I had to devise another means to exact retribution on you today."

She didn't flinch, but her pupils narrowed and she tensed. She was a little warrior, in the complete opposite way he was. The kind who remained alert to all dangers, bending but never breaking.

He shifted the sitting platform to the middle of the room and sank into it. "Take off the shirt."

She pulled it over her head in one fluid motion and tossed it on the floor, in a small show of defiance.

His lips twitched. "Pick that up and fold it neatly, pet. You know I won't tolerate insolence."

Something deadened behind her eyes and he regretted whatever he'd said that had triggered her emotional shutdown. He definitely didn't want her disengaged.

"Or rather," he tried to fix it, "I'll punish you for insolence. That doesn't mean I don't expect it now and then."

It worked. She returned, curiosity flickering behind her eyes. "What made you like this? How did you learn you liked..." she swallowed, seeming unable to finish.

"To punish?" He smiled. "I had a lover—Depri's sister, actually. She loved pain. Loved to have control forced away from her, to be held down and hurt in a way that didn't cause lasting harm."

"What happened to her?"

He knew she'd ask the question, and braced himself for the sharp jab that always lanced through him when he thought of it. This time, though, it seemed less painful than usual. "She was killed during a transaction." To the day he died he would regret not going instead of her. It should have been him who had fallen that day.

Lily paled. "I'm sorry," she murmured.

He shrugged. "It's been a long time. Almost four solar cycles now." He needed to redirect this conversation before his mood went south. "But I learned many things with her. How to torture a female in the ways that fulfill the most." He flashed a wicked, promising smile. "Now lie over my lap."

Her eyebrows lifted. "I thought you weren't going to spank me."

He grinned. "That doesn't mean I don't still own your ass. So when I say bend over, you'd better obey quickly, pet, or I'll make the punishment more challenging that it already will be."

A shiver visibly ran through her, but she did as he commanded, gingerly folding herself over his thighs and presenting her perfect little ass.

"Reach back and pull open your cheeks."

"What?" He sensed more confusion than disobedience in her tone.

"You heard me."

She shot him a questioning look, but reached her hands back and prised her cheeks apart.

He unwrapped the root and worked the freshly peeled end, which he'd carved in the shape of a finger, against her anus.

She clenched her back pucker, tightening her ass.

He slapped the back of her thigh. "Do you need a spanking, too?"

"No." He loved the sulleness in her tone.

He popped each cheek once, anyway. "Open up." Wiggling the end of the root against her back entrance, he applied steady pressure.

She gasped when it breached her tight muscles and entered. He pushed it in until he reached the end he'd notched to keep it from entering all the way inside.

"Now stand up." He gave her ass a pat.

She stood up, the little root sticking out from between her ass cheeks. Soon it would begin to produce heat, even burning.

"Straddle my knees," he ordered.

She adjusted and started to climb onto his lap, straddling him, but he held her back with a hand at her hips. "Not sitting. Standing." He lowered his knees, hoping she'd manage it.

"Oh." She lifted her weight onto her feet, which forced her legs to be spread wide.

"Good, pet." Her bare breasts bobbed right in front of his face, her pussy was spread between his legs and the spicy root he'd inserted protruded from her ass. The sight was so erotic, so lovely, he wanted to capture it forever.

He reached behind her and pumped the root in and out of her ass, watching her face flush and nostrils flare.

"What is that?"

"Anal punishment."

She tossed him a suspicious look—probably guessing there was more to it than that.

"You'll find out soon enough."

Wariness scrawled over her visage.

"Your bottom is too sore, but there are other parts of you I can spank. Can you guess what they are?"

Her belly fluttered with a rasped breath. "No." Her voice was little more than a whisper.

He slapped her left breast with a quick, arcing open palm.

She jumped and moved to step back, but he caught her waist. "Ah ah. Where are you going? You stay right here for your punishment." He slapped her right breast.

Her breath quickened, making her breasts rise and fall at an alluring rate.

He yanked her forward, and applied his mouth to her left nipple, twirling his tongue around her nipple, scraping his teeth across the delicate flesh, then sucking it into his mouth. The moment he released it, he slapped his fingers across it again, watching it bounce under his treatment.

"Which is better? Breasts or..." He clapped his palm up between her legs, connecting with her wet, plump folds. "Pussy?"

She cried out, wobbling, but he held her up with the hand on her hip.

"You've been naughty, pet. Your pretty little pussy deserves to be punished." He slapped it again. "So does this ass." He pumped the root in her anus.

"Oh." Her startled look told him that the root had begun to heat inside her.

He slapped her pussy again, which dripped with arousal. "I told you I would punish you every day until we reach Ocretia. I wouldn't lie. If your ass is still too sore tomorrow, I'll tie your legs open and whip those inner thighs until you scream for mercy."

The wariness had gone from her face, replaced by desire. Her eyes glowed glassy, breath came in pants. "Please," she breathed.

He screwed two fingers inside her hot channel and watched her face. Judging from the way her muscles contracted around his fingers, she was ready to blow.

He shoved down his flight pants, allowing his cock to spring free. "Climb on it."

The relief in her expression was almost comical. Or it would have been if his own desperation didn't match hers. He gripped her ass and impaled her on his cock, unable to wait for her trembling movement.

She gasped at the sudden intrusion. He let her adjust to his size by pumping that wicked root in and out of her ass, twisting and turning it to renew the burn.

"Oh stars, oh *veck*," she moaned, rocking her hips up to meet his.

He nearly died from the rightness of it.

"That's it, beautiful. Take me deeper," he growled, moving her hips forward and back over his erection, using the length of his cock to rub her clit each time she moved out.

"Oh *veck!*" Her gaze flew around, a frantic wild quality to her movements now.

He took her right nipple into his mouth and sucked hard, still yanking her in and out over his cock so fast her teeth probably rattled.

The sound of her gasping breath, the desperation of her gyrating hips sent him over the edge. His thighs tensed, balls contracted. Stars danced before his eyes.

"Come, Lily," he roared, unable to wait for her.

He yanked her body against his and held her tight, his cock buried deep inside her as he came and came.

She, too, found her release, shudders bucking through her lithe body until she lay limp as a rag doll.

He bit the place where her shoulder met her neck and laid a kiss behind her ear. To his surprise, she pushed off his lap, limbs jerky with anger.

Oh *veck*. Had he hurt her? A sheet of cold doused his body.

~.~

Lily stalked away to face the corner, arms crossed over her chest, shoulders hunched.

Get it together, Lily. Get it together.

Tears burned in her eyes and her heart jumped erratically in her chest.

What had just happened? She'd never lost control like that. *Veck,* had she ever even been present during sex before?

"Lily?" She heard Rok surge to his feet behind her, and his two beefy forearms appeared on either side of her, caging her against the wall.

"*Veck*, Lily. Did I hurt you?"

The shocked concern in his voice only made the restless emotions ricocheting through her body worse. She had to get a grip on them before she unravelled completely.

When she didn't answer or turn, he shifted to catch her shoulders. "I went too far. I'm sorry."

His apology only ratcheted up her confusion. Why did he care about her feelings? Wasn't this supposed to be retribution for her crimes against him? The icy truth that her suspicion it was something altogether different sent her tumbling headlong down the mountain of uncertainty.

What was this male playing at? And why—by the Earth's one true moon—*why* did he have such an effect on her?

He turned her slowly and the soft regret on his face undid her.

"Get off me," she shouted, shoving his hands away. "I don't know what you're playing at, but I want no part of it."

"Tell me what I did. Why are you angry with me?"

Because it wasn't what he'd done, but this very concern that had her chest in shreds, she slapped his face.

He let her. Yes, she actually saw him start to withdraw the target, then let the slap fall. But he'd had enough. He caught both her wrists and yanked her against his chest.

"Did you like it too much?" his face was grim and the knowing in his tone nearly dropped her to the floor.

Tears spilled down her cheeks like a valve had opened.

Rok caught her around the waist, holding her up. He plucked out the vegetable that burned and heated her ass, leaving her entire pelvic region warm, her pussy dripping. Even after that vigorous ride, after taking his huge Zandian cock, she wanted more.

And it terrified her.

She shouldn't desire her captor. Find pleasure with her master. Receive comfort from the male who planned to give her over to her death in just a few weeks.

This maelstrom of conflicting emotions made it impossible for her to think, to reason her way out of this bizarre entrapment with a tender captor who liked to cause her pain.

Except she hadn't noticed the pain because the driving force of the need, the *vecking* edge he'd had her on all planet rotation had her begging him for it. And the humiliation of it all—the burning root which he'd pumped relentlessly in and out of her ass, the pussy spanking, the breast spanking—it all replayed in her mind so loudly, in such vivid detail and color and sensation that she couldn't *breathe*.

This wasn't her.

Rok scooped her into his arms and slid her onto the sleeping platform. He popped a tube in a liquid pack and pressed it to her lips. "Drink."

She hadn't known she was thirsty, but the sweet liquid cooled her mouth and throat. She pulled hard, swallowing in quick bursts until she'd finished the entire pack.

"Look at me." Rok stood beside the platform, a crease between his brows. His shirt was off and his bare chest rippled with muscle.

She obeyed.

"Are you hurt?" he asked the question slowly and clearly, as if her answer was of the utmost importance.

She shook her head.

"Did I take things too far?"

She couldn't bring herself to say yes. It hovered on her lips, both a truth and a lie.

She dropped to her side, offering her back, and stared at the wall.

"Oh no, you don't." Rok caught her upper arm and rolled her over to face him. "Don't you *dare* turn wax doll on me, Lily. Not after that *vecking spectacular* display of sensuality. Sexuality—whatever. We're going to talk about this. You liked it. I know you liked it," he said fiercely, as if the universe depended on him convincing both of them. He brought his palms to her face, bracketing it with a soft touch. "It was intense for me, too."

Her breath stalled. Stuttered. Stalled again. Their gazes locked, his amethyst eyes boring down into hers, nothing but dead sincerity on his handsome face.

After a long moment, he flicked off the light. "I'm going to crawl up there beside you and if there's anything you want to tell me in the dark, while you don't have to look at me, I'll be listening."

Her heart hammered against her ribs. What did he think she would say? What was he inviting her to say?

She had no experience to help her navigate this male, nor the feelings still swimming around her gut.

He laid down beside her, catching and tying her wrists so easily in the dark she wondered if she was the only one who couldn't see. The blackness did provide some measure of safety, though it also seemed to give her emotions room to expand, which she didn't like.

"I got scared," she admitted.

Rok slid his hand across her breast in a light caress. "You haven't let go before."

She considered his words, plopped like stepping stones in front of her, to help her find the way out of the hole she'd descended into. "No, I haven't."

"I did humiliating things to you and you're not sure how you feel about that."

Even as her insides squeezed in the agony of embarrassment, her pussy clenched. "Yes," she whispered. This might be the crux of the problem. Her sexual response was not in line with her mental one. "Why do you enjoy that?" she snarled. "Hurting and humiliating females?"

"Lily...If you hadn't responded, if you'd cried or begged me to stop, if you'd turned to stone, as I've seen you do, I would've stopped. But you liked it. Your pussy dripped for me. You begged me to take you."

Her face grew warm in the darkness. Yes, she had begged him.

"Is that what you like? The begging?"

"I love all of it, pet. I love being in charge. I love frightening you. Hurting you. I love making you cry and then I love making it better."

She curled into a tight ball on her side. "That's just wrong."

The light came back on and she yelped from the intensity, blinking at the sheet of white blared across her vision. "Very well." His clipped voice made her sit up and pay attention.

He stood from the bed and made an impatient gesture. "Get up."

"Why?" Her heart thudded, somehow it knew this consequence

would be her worst yet, and it wasn't going to involve pain. At least not the physical kind.

"I'll lock you in a different room. You can stay there until we arrive in Ocretian territory." His expression was closed and stony. She saw the warrior in him now—huge, fierce. Terrifying. Not a being she'd want to cross.

Cold waves of panic ran through her. "No." Her rational mind said she needed to stick with Rok if she wanted any chance of escape. Her heart screamed the same. Her insides had dropped to the floor, leaving her an empty shell, cold and paper thin, ready to blow away at Rok's next breath.

He arched a brow. "No?"

She shook from head to foot. Since her rational mind had left, she reverted to her training, dropping to her knees at his feet, bowing her head low. "Forgive me, master."

He hauled her back up so quickly she yelped. He lifted her by her upper arms, until they saw eye-to-eye, her feet dangling in the air.

"Ouch," she squirmed. Somehow she knew this wasn't one of the ways he meant to hurt her.

She was right. He dropped her like she'd scalded him and stepped back. His eyes burned dark purple with anger.

She wanted to rub her arms, knowing there'd be finger bruises there soon, but her bound wrists made it impossible. She tried it less formally this time. "I'm sorry, Rok. Please don't send me from your chamber. I won't complain of your treatment of me again."

But that still wasn't what he wanted to hear. He put his hand to the screen and his door slid open. "Let's go." The coldness in his expression cut her like a blade.

Her throat closed and her nose burned. She thrust her jaw forward. "No, I won't go. I belong here. For your punishment."

He remained wooden. No, stone. "Don't feed me what you think I want to hear."

She winced and held her breath to keep from crying. "I'm speaking the truth. You were right. I like what you do to me. Maybe too much."

There. That was the most raw veracity she knew.

The harsh lines of Rok's face gentled, though he didn't move.

"My ass isn't really sore," she admitted. "—it just looks bad. You could spank me tonight..." The heat of a flush crept up her neck.

Rok stared at her for a long moment. Then the corners of his lips twitched and he cupped her nape, dragging her up against his huge, hard body and pressing his lips to her hair. "It's not sore, hmm?"

"Not so much. A few twinges now and then."

"I'll punish you for that deception, too, then. Tomorrow."

The door swished shut as he released his hold on the hand-panel. He spun her around to face the sleeping platform and forced her torso down. She held her breath, waiting. He'd said tomorrow for the spanking, so what was this? More sex?

But his huge palm clapped down on her ass, landing a flurry of spanks that send her to her toes. Six, seven, eight. He stopped and rubbed her screaming flesh.

"Tomorrow I'm going to fuck this pretty little ass. Teach you to mean it when you call me master."

~.~

ROK SCOOPED his little human onto the sleeping platform and crawled in beside her, wrapping an arm over her waist and molding her soft body against his. Despite the difference in their sizes, in their species, she nested perfectly with him.

He hit the button on the wall behind his head to extinguish the artificial light in the room. He hated that weak light—his cells longing for the crystal amplified sunlight Zandia had featured.

"Is that why you don't like when I call you master?"

His chest closed, the ache every time she said that word automatic. Taraw had called him that, with complete surrender and total submission. She'd look up at him with adoration, waiting for his command.

"*She* called you that."

He sucked in a breath, startled. Did the human read minds like Mierna?

"Who?"

"Depri's sister. You never said her name."

"Taraw. Yes."

Silence stretched between them as his throat closed with grief and guilt. "I'm sorry for your loss."

He couldn't speak. Taraw had been as different from Lily as a female could be. Willowy and tall, like Depri, she'd been a warrior, as forceful as any. Only on the sleeping platform did she surrender. Lily had been a slave, trained in subservience, but she resisted her real surrender. That was the part that had frightened her earlier.

"I've never loved anyone." Her voice sounded hollow. The emptiness of it scraped at his chest.

"No?" The image of her sister and mother's faces, pinched with concern over her flashed in his mind. "No family? Friends?"

"None. The closest I came to friends were those slaves I escaped with. But…"

"But what?"

"Things turned divisive with them almost as soon as we settled. There wasn't enough food to go around. Things were hard. We took care of each other, but there was a lot of infighting and resentment."

"What happened to them?"

"An explosion hit the camp. I was out foraging for food. We weren't supposed to be out alone, but I'd needed some time away. I was still enjoying my freedom." The bitterness in her voice made him wince.

But she wasn't a slave anymore, not really. If she didn't realize that yet, she would soon. Even more when she was reunited with her mother and sister. He smiled, knowing she couldn't see him in the darkness. Giving her that gift—one she'd never had, or could no longer remember—would be sweet.

4

Lily woke in Rok's chamber just as mixed up as she'd been the night before. The lights were on half-strength and she was alone, but he'd moved a hover seat close to the bed and a plate of food sat upon it.

Her heart squeezed uncomfortably. She wasn't even sure why. Just because Rok had been thoughtful enough to leave food? Or was it something more?

She'd been broken, but not in any way a master had broken her before. Last night Rok had made her *choose* to stay with him. Choose to submit to his punishment, to serve as his sex slave. And she had chosen.

As much as she'd like to believe she'd chosen with her cool, rational mind, because staying with Rok offered greater chance of escape, deep down, she knew it wasn't true.

It went far deeper.

She needed to see where this thing with Rok was going. To understand the emotions he stirred in her, as disturbing as they may be. She spent the morning trying to identify them and came up with one word: need.

He created desire in her—not just for his touch, for sexual

release, but also for his attention, his approval, his nearness. She wanted to be with him at all times, to watch the grace of his hulking body in motion, to admire the easy command he had of his ship and crew. Because they didn't act subservient to him, yet they all still deferred.

They'd chosen him too.

A tingle ran through her when she realized it. This was the sort of master he was. The kind others choose to follow, not because they are forced by station or threat of punishment, but because he is the one who leads best.

It brought home the problem that plagued the escaped slaves—lack of a clear, trusted leader. They'd all been so eager to be free, to follow their own will, they couldn't get organized around any authority. Decision-making had been impossible, because the group wouldn't even agree to a democratic rule of majority vote for each decision.

The night before, when she'd realized his dead lover called him master, jealousy had gutted her. She'd swallowed back the hurt because his pain was palpable, but it sent up such a longing for what he'd had, for what they'd had together, she could scarcely breathe.

Love.

The only inkling she had of its meaning was when she tried to conjure up a picture of her parents. Though no specific memories came up, she was certain she'd been loved. She had known love, once.

The beings who hadn't—girls brought to the training institute as infants—never could be trusted. They never made friends with the other girls or helped each other out. She had had friends there.

She'd forgotten in that moment of self-pity the night before when she said she'd never known love.

Though the trainers separated any slaves they suspected of forming bonds with each other, the children had formed bonds, nonetheless. They comforted each other after punishments, protected one another's emotions and souls, even when they couldn't protect each other's physical bodies.

Remembering them renewed in her the vision that had died on Jesel—a free human race. She still believed it could be done, wanted to participate in the liberation of her people.

It strengthened her resolve. She did still have a purpose beyond her own basic survival. She must escape and find a way to help others to escape. There had to be a way. If only she could stop Rok's craft from entering Ocretion airspace.

She knew nothing about spacecrafts, but maybe there was a way to disable this one—enough that he'd have to land somewhere sooner than later. Create a slow leak in the fuel supply, perhaps.

She climbed off the sleeping platform and pulled Rok's shirt on. She liked that he'd worn it, that it belonged to him.

Like she did.

No—he wasn't keeping her. Was that what made her heart squelch so? She'd finally been claimed by a master whose touch she actually *wanted*—craved, actually—but he didn't have any interest in keeping her around? Worse, he planned to send her to her death so he could claim the bounty on her head.

Jagged pain slashed her chest. She had to escape. Either that, or she had to make him change her mind. Somehow, escaping seemed the less daunting task.

She ate the food. It had the deadened taste of food that had been reconstituted, but wasn't horrible. She wondered what and when Rok ate.

The door slid open and the alien in question leaned against the frame, looking sexy as hell in a black, skin tight undershirt and matching black flight pants. His gaze fell on her, cool and assessing.

"How are you feeling?"

A riot of emotions rippled through her. She realized she didn't know her role. He didn't like when she "played" at slave, nor could she bring out the steely revolutionary who'd stolen his ship. She didn't owe him anger after the kindness he'd shown her the night before.

Thankfully, he let her off without answering. "Care for a shower this morning? I imagine you need the washroom at least."

She exhaled. "Yes, please. That would be wonderful." A new shyness made it too difficult to look at his face, so she settled into her usual slave-gaze in the direction of his feet.

He caught her chin when she approached and lifted it. His expression held curiosity and he seemed to see right into her soul. She shifted on her feet and swallowed.

He lowered his head and brushed his lips across hers.

She went still. A kiss. The tenderness of it rocked her right down to her bare feet.

Rok groaned against her mouth and shifted the hand at her chin to the back of her head, holding her still as he deepened the kiss. His other hand gripped her ass, squeezing hard.

She lifted her thigh to wrap it around his legs and he immediately palmed her entire ass and lifted it higher, until her core met the hardened bulge of his cock through the flight pants.

"*Veck*, little girl. I'm hard for you already." He inhaled deeply with his face at her neck. "Your scent drives me mad. You'd best get to the washroom fast before I decide you need a hard *veck* up against this wall first."

She wasn't sure she *didn't* need a hard *veck* up against the wall first, but her bladder protested so she ducked past Rok and padded toward the washroom.

~.~

Rok waited for his little slave to emerge from the washroom, her freshly washed skin just as intoxicating in scent as it had been before her cleaning. She still wore his shirt, which he adored on her.

"Have you ever played walnees?" he asked.

Her blank look told him she had not.

"It's a strategy game. Come, I'll teach you. It's fun." But as he led her to the exercise/game room, the lights flashed a warning amber and the mechanical voice of the flight computer announced, "Approaching space debris. Repeat, approaching space debris. Adjust flight course immediately."

He grabbed Lily's hand and they sprinted to the flight controls. Mierna was already snapping her safety harness in place in the co-pilot's seat.

Janu and Jaso sped around the corner, followed by Gaurdo and Depri.

"Everyone buckle in," he barked and shoved Lily into a seat, yanking the harness down around her.

"I've got it." She snatched the buckle from his hands and fastened it for herself.

"Activate protective shields," he barked at Mierna.

"Already on it," she sang out.

He slid into his seat, buckling with one hand as his other reached to flick on manual control. Taking the directional knobs, he dodged the debris flying at the ship from all sides, jumping to the right, then left, swooping around, flipping to fly sideways between two large pieces. Smaller pieces hit off the outside of the ship, sounding far worse than they probably actually were. In his experience, the space junk had to be big and heavy enough to throw them off course when it hit to cause any external damage. So far, he'd avoided those largest pieces.

But the debris field became thicker.

"Fastest way out is 120 degrees," Mierna reported. "But the debris is thickest in that direction."

He angled north, but almost immediately dropped back down to avoid smashing the ship. "Negative. Too hostile. What are my other options?" He slowed their speed to navigate the heavy influx of space trash.

"Incoming," Mierna shouted. "Spacecraft, appears unfriendly."

"Gaurdo and Depri, prepare to fire on my command." He kept his clipped tones calm, although it appeared they were under attack. Space pirates sometimes used the cover of debris to lie in wait.

"Three more—shots fired."

He dodged the laser fire from the first ship, swung around and lined his ship up to fire back. "Fire at will," he commanded.

His world narrowed to the razor sharp reflexes necessary to maneuver the ship in and out of debris and enemy fire. "Take the *veckers* down," he growled when he provided a straight shot for his crew to fire.

Their laser fire hit the enemy ship and it exploded in a burst of flames. Immediately, the three other ships charged his, obviously intent on revenge.

He dropped straight down, swerving around a piece of debris. Unfortunately, a huge piece caught the top of the craft, sending them into a spin. With a curse, he wrestled the controls to ease the ship out of the spin.

Laser fire struck their shields on the starboard side.

He flipped the ship one hundred and eighty degrees, making them hover upside down directly in front of one of the enemy ships.

Jano and Jaso fired on the ship and it exploded into flames, blinding him.

He eased off the speed and righted the craft. The other two enemy ships retreated. An alarm bell sounded, signalling damage to the craft.

Gaurdo unbuckled from his seat. "I'll look at it," he rumbled.

Rok dipped the craft to the right, finally escaping the field of debris.

"Clear," Mierna reported.

He shoved the thrust to full throttle and the ship sped forward out of the treacherous territory. "Status, Gaurdo?" he sent his voice through to Gaurdo's flight collar.

"Not yet," came his gruff reply.

"Are we talking life-threatening damage?"

"No."

The rest of the crew unbuckled and left the cockpit, presumably to help Gaurdo.

He glanced over his shoulder. An unfamiliar urge to protect the female behind him made him itchy over the damage to the ship. Lily's lovely face had gone pale, but it was the look in her eyes that made his heart stall in his chest.

She appeared to be in awe...*of him.*

"Where'd you learn to fly like that?" She moistened her lips with that pretty little tongue of hers.

He shrugged. "Always flown. It's all I know how to do."

"You know how to fight."

Her insistence on being impressed by him made something lodge in his throat. Though he'd never sought meaning or purpose in his life, some odd desire to become or do something more rose up in him.

"All I know how to do is lie down and take it."

The bitterness in her voice shredded him. A great, dark anger surged within him at all the idiot masters she'd had who hadn't seen her as a being. Hadn't treasured her. He'd be *vecked* if he wasn't going to try to show her something different.

"Come here." He beckoned to her.

Surprise flitted over her face and her fingers fumbled at her harness. When it popped free, she came to him. It pleased him how easily she obeyed—and not out of fear. She was beginning to trust him.

He pulled her down onto his lap and buried his face in her neck, breathing in the scent of her silky hair. "You want to learn how to fly?"

She pulled back, eyebrows raised. "Really?"

He shrugged. "We both know you're capable of far more than lying down and taking it. You're intelligent. You're quick. And you know how to follow the path of least resistance."

Her blush made him want to take her long and hard just to prove he'd meant it, but he restrained his desire. This moment was for Lily to be something other than a receptacle, for once. "Let's start with flying a ship. That way, the next time you steal some idiot's ship, you won't have to crash land it."

She choked on a laugh. He swore light beamed from her face, her smile was so bright. He arranged her on his lap and placed her hands on the controls, explaining what each one did.

"It's not on autopilot now, so any movements you make will be real. Go ahead and try it."

"But is the ship okay? We're not going to lose a wing or anything are we?"

"If we do, I promise I'll take over." He grinned.

She shifted the directional thrust and the ship wobbled, one wing dipping.

"Help!" she gasped.

He covered her hand and nudged the plane back into balance. "It's touchy, but you get the feel of it after a while."

Gaurdo's voice came through on his collar. "There's been damage to the outer shell. We won't make it to Ocretian airspace. We'll have to stop sooner."

He cursed. "How much sooner?"

"Two to four planet rotations."

"Mierna, research possible landing locations."

"Already working on it," she sang out, implying she'd already known this outcome.

Lily shifted and settled on his lap, sending his cock into false expectations about what they were doing.

Soon, he'd *veck* her. She was his to take any time he liked. But right now, he loved her pleasure and delight.

~.~

AFTER SHOWING her how to fly and feeding her a mid-day meal, Rok led her to his chamber and pulled her only covering—his thin undershirt—off her. His gaze dropped to her nipples, which tightened the moment his horns stiffened and his lids drooped.

Rok didn't miss the change. "They're begging for my mouth, aren't they?"

Heat flooded her core.

He tweaked on between his thumb and finger, pinching just hard enough to make her lips part. "You'll have to beg me for that later, little human. Right now, I want you to make yourself comfortable with your fingers between your legs. You get that pussy nice and slick for me, because when I come back, it needs to be wet and ready. Understand?"

She didn't understand, not really. The instructions, yes, but not his game. But she nodded anyway. "Yes, master."

His gaze sharpened and he studied her face, perhaps searching for her sincerity. She thought she'd meant it, but whatever he saw didn't convince him. His eyes narrowed. "Don't call me that," he growled. "I'll punish you when I return."

She didn't experience dread at that promise. More of a morbid curiosity bordering on excitement. Whe wondered what more the sadistic alien had in mind for her.

He left her in his chamber.

She climbed on the sleeping platform and gingerly reached down to touch between her legs. The truth was that she had no experience with pleasuring herself. It had been forbidden at the training institute, and afterward, she'd never had an interest. She'd spent most of her time disassociated from those parts of her body—from all of her body, really.

Until Rok, she'd never known pleasure of any kind.

She explored her folds with a sort of scientific curiosity. What made her wet and ready? Unpleasant memories of being used while completely dry and ill-prepared rushed in and a wave of nausea made her stop.

She couldn't do this.

She would allow Rok to do whatever he wanted with her, but she wouldn't willingly pleasure herself. She just didn't need that sort of thing.

She put her arms stiffly by her sides and closed her eyes,

removing herself from her body and the situation she didn't know how to handle.

She didn't know how long it took Rok to return—her sense of time had floated away with her mind.

He frowned when he saw her position on the bed.

She sat up quickly.

"Spread your legs and show me your pussy."

She bent her knees and opened her feet wide.

"Is she wet for me?" Rok crossed the small space and dragged his thumb across her slit. It caught in her folds. He raised an eyebrow. "What happened?"

Sullenness stole over her—an unfamiliar emotion. Certainly one she'd never allowed herself to reveal to a master. "I didn't know how," she said stiffly.

"No?" Only polite surprise tinged his voice. "I'll show you, then." He climbed onto the platform and sat with his back against the wall. After widening his legs, he grasped her around the waist and pulled her back flush against his front, her buttocks nested against the bulge in his flight pants.

He tapped her clitoris lightly with the pad of his index finger. "You know about this spot, I presume." *Tap, tap, tap.*

Her sluggish sexuality sputtered back to life, blood rushing to the area.

"Did you touch yourself here?"

"No."

He slapped her pussy and she yelped, squeezing her thighs around his hand.

"Naughty, slave." He picked her knees up and draped them over the outsides of his legs, so they were pinned wide open. "Keep them here or there will be consequences. I expect your full cooperation with your punishments."

He slapped her pussy again.

She sucked her breath in across her teeth and threw her head back on his shoulder.

"When I tell you to prepare yourself," he spanked her poor sex with even, firm slaps, "I expect you to obey me." He delivered five more and swiped the pad of his finger across her sex.

This time it slid easily, her natural lubricant flowing.

"That's better," he murmured, spreading the moisture up to her clit and tracing a slow, torturous circle around it.

"Maybe all you need is my punishment to get you hot."

She flushed. That couldn't be true, could it? Yet she couldn't remember ever growing moist before.

He flipped her around so she lay across his lap, then threaded her hand underneath her hips and between her legs. "Stroke yourself, beautiful. Keep it wet while I spank you."

She touched her sex, surprised at how plump and swollen her folds had grown.

Rok brought his palm down on her right cheek, hard.

She yelped and curled her fingers back into her hand, bracing for the pain.

Though the hand was underneath her, somehow he knew. He slapped the back of her leg, which hurt even worse, and reached around to replace her fingers. With his digits tangled over the top of hers, he gave her a quick tutorial on how to touch herself, making a tight circle over her clit, then thrusting a finger inside her.

"Keep it going or I'll spank down here." He popped her thigh again.

"No," she shrieked.

He chuckled. "Be a good pet, then. Do as you're told. I need you to learn how to pleasure yourself."

Her head swam, as if the concept itself made her dizzy. A master ordering her to pleasure herself was a most bizarre and backward experience. Fingers fluttering between her legs, she tensed her shoulders, every cell in her body listening intently to the sensations created from simultaneous spanking and masturbation.

He spanked with a heavy hand, slow, measured strokes, without any rubbing or petting in between. The steady and predictable cadence helped her settle into the pain, accepting it, even though it set her bottom on fire.

After what seemed like an endless duration, Rok picked up speed.

She cried out in protest, but he once more set up a rhythm, just twice as fast as the last one. Her own fingers picked up the pace as well, matching his thorough spanking with a frantic, jerky pulse. Need coiled inside her, dark and hot. The sensations mingled, pain and desperate desire.

"Rok," she gasped, hips bobbing on his lap—whether they were reaching to meet his hand or move away from it, she wasn't sure.

"That's it, beautiful." His voice sounded deeper than usual. "Say my name when you come, say it."

"Rok...Rok!" she shrieked. All the muscles in her pelvic floor tightened. Her thighs tightened, squeezing her hand tightly between them, her butt cheeks clenched. Under her fingers, her pelvic floor contracted six, seven times. All the while, Rok kept spanking her, even harder now, and so fast that the sensations exploded into one giant tumultuously satisfying event.

She lost track of time, of herself, of everything. Not in the way she normally "went out" during sex. Not like that at all. She felt only pleasure—glorious, satisfying. Bone-deep.

When awareness came filtering back in, she was lying, collapsed over Rok's lap, with his large hand running slow circles over her flaming ass.

"Rok," she croaked.

Once more, she wanted to cry. Not out of sadness. Not out of humiliation or frustration or anger. Not for any reason other than that she felt wrung out. Maybe that had been what happened last night, too.

A blanket fell around her shoulders and when Rok rolled her up against his torso, she was cradled like a baby.

"Good, pet. Sweet, beautiful female."

She squeezed her eyes closed and tucked her face into his chest, unable to bear looking at him.

"I'm going to let you hide for about ten more seconds and then you're going to let me look in your eyes so I can see what's going on."

Another mini-orgasm ran through her at that. This new brand of mastery, of dominance which demanded she bare her soul, not just surrender her body, gave him a terrible power over her.

A terrible, wonderful power.

Her body began to shake and Rok wrapped her up tighter. Her eyes fluttered open.

"You're fine, beautiful. They're just aftershocks. It will pass soon. I've got you." He offered her a tube of sweet fluid, which she sipped.

"I have something that might help, actually. A human food—medicinal—originally from Earth." He rocked her close. "After the shakes go away, I'll get you some."

Tears burned behind her eyes. *Veck.* She didn't want to cry—not again. She struggled to keep it in, holding her breath, but Rok gripped her chin and tipped her face up to his. "Are you crying again?"

She shook her head but the torrent released in a ridiculous snort-sob, tears leaking from both eyes.

He wrapped his hand around the side of her head and kissed her hair. "Let's get you that treat."

She pressed her body against him, not wanting him to put her down, but he seemed to understand. He climbed off the bed with her cradled in his arms, then swung her around to carry her on one hip, like a child carried by a parent.

She felt ridiculous and tall and pleased all at once. A giggle escaped her lips.

Rok smiled up at her, his violet eyes warm.

Her chest swelled so large she thought it would burst.

He carried her to a cabinet, which he unlocked with his palm print on the panel. Inside were stacks and stacks of black bricks. "I received them in trade. I'd planned to sell them to the wealthy in Ocretia, but once I tasted it, decided to keep it for myself." He unwrapped one brick, sliced the end off it and popped it in her mouth.

She puckered at the bitterness and made a face. "I think it's gone bad."

He shook his head. "No, it hasn't, it's just better sweetened. I'll make you a nice drink with it, later, but let this melt on your tongue. You'll be restored in no time."

She let the bitter dark slice dissolve in her mouth. "What's it called?"

He grinned. "Chocolate. It was considered a food of the gods and an elixir of life in ancient human civilizations. You ought to know these things—" He'd been teasing, but he broke off, probably realizing she'd have no chance to know anything about her species as a slave. "I'm sorry," he muttered. "Of course you wouldn't know."

Her body began to hum, energy from the chocolate enlivening her.

"You're feeling it."

She'd never had a master—or any other being for that matter—pay so much attention to her. It was addictive—more heady than the chocolate buzzing through her veins.

To reward her thoughtful master, she gripped one of his horns and sank her mouth down on the other one.

"Holy *veck*," he growled, lurching and sending her unbalanced weight careening in a circle. "Little girl, you have exactly twenty planet rotations to stop that."

She gave a husky laugh, her mouth still stretched wide over his horn. Her tongue laved the side of his horn, lips suctioned over it.

"Veeeeck, little pet." The arm under her ass boosted her higher. The position was perfect, as she sat high above his head and it was easy to angle her mouth down around the frisky horns.

"Other side, other side, other side," he rasped. He'd leaned his hip against the sleeping platform and had his free hand in his flight pants, stroking his length.

She switched horns, staring at his enormous malehood when he pulled it from his pants. It grew, a drop of rainbow pre-cum glistening on the tip. She wanted to have that huge organ in her mouth instead.

"Do you want me to suck him instead?"

Rok groaned. "Yes—no. *Veck*, I don't know. I wish there were two of you." His slipping control encouraged her and took the bite away from the insinuation that she wasn't enough on her own. "Lily..." He made a quick reverse, so his opposite hip faced the sleeping platform—the one with her on it. She climbed onto her knees, the blanket that had hung around her shoulders falling down.

She worked faster, using both hands now—one on each horn, her tongue switching between each stiffened protuberance.

He barked a curse, then thrust her away.

Her momentary offense drained away when she saw the dark lust in his eyes. He shoved her to her ass, then pushed her on her back and dragged one horn down the center of her naked body, groaning the entire time.

When he reached her core, he rubbed her clit clumsily with the horn, then switched his head and penetrated her with the other one.

She gasped and gripped his free horn, pulling his head up, disappointed when the horn did not sink deep enough inside her to satisfy.

"Roll over." His deep gravelly voice reverberated through her entire body. "I told you I'd take this luscious little ass today. The time has come." The swish of his palm over her still heated skin made her arch her bottom up to him and purr.

He moved from the sleeping platform and she watched him walk to one of the cabinets, his huge member bobbing in front of him. A pang of anxiety twisted.

He would never fit.

Not her in her anus.

He returned with a jar of some kind of oil or salve which he slathered over his enormous cock.

"Rok...I don't think...it's too big."

"I don't think it's too big, either." He smirked, deliberately misunderstanding her. "It's punishment, remember, pet? You'll have to stretch to let me in. You'll find full surrender when I master you this way, little slave."

Her anxiety only ratcheted higher, but she didn't dare argue with him.

He stuffed two pillows under her hips to raise her backside. "Hold your cheeks open, pet. I'm going to *veck* you until you scream."

His words did not reassure.

Her fingers twisted into the worn fabric of the platform covering. *Please don't hurt me.*

"Lily." His voice cracked with sharp command.

She jumped, then replayed his previous command in her mind, listening this time. Reluctantly, she opened, realizing the full humiliation of holding her own ass wide for his plunder.

He rubbed some of the lubricant on her anus.

She closed her eyes and did what she did best—disappear. Drop out of her body and hang in limbo, somewhere else. No—nowhere.

Rok nudged her rear hole with the head of his cock and she observed it, as if from far away—noticing, but with complete detachment.

"Lily." The sharpened tone brought her back again.

What command had she failed to obey now?

Abruptly, her world spun and she found herself on her back, looking into Rok's angry face.

"Where did you go?"

She blinked at him. *Vecking* excrement. This male was far too perceptive.

"Don't you dare go dead on me like that. You think I want to *veck* a wax doll?"

Figuring the question was rhetorical, she didn't answer. Or maybe it was because she hadn't fully returned.

Rok picked up her ankles and held them in the air with one hand, leaving his other hand free to punish her. He slapped her ass, the backs of her legs and her exposed pussy with hard, attention-demanding spanks. The poisoned bite on her ankle throbbed but Rok hadn't noticed it.

All her numbness dissipated as the shock of each stinging slap set her nerves on fire.

"Rok, please," she gasped, twisting her hips to dodge the blows to no avail.

The moment he stopped spanking her, his thumb penetrated her ass, sinking to the knuckle.

The invasion wasn't nearly so unpleasant as she'd expected. In fact, her pussy pulsed, clenching and releasing on air with excitement.

"You don't want my cock in this ass?" he growled, pumping his thumb inside her. "This ass that I own for the next twenty planet rotations?"

"I..." Her tongue worked in her dry mouth. She couldn't quite bring herself to admit she wanted it, but flames licked her core, need growing larger.

"Look at me." His voice snapped like a whip.

She gazed around her legs at him.

He removed his thumb from her ass and she registered its loss with disappointment.

"Don't look away." The command came softly this time. He pulled open her cheeks and pushed his cock against her anus. Her feet found his shoulders and he wrapped his huge hands around the fronts of her thighs to brace her for his thrust.

She whimpered her protest, not daring to move as he stretched her wide. "Rok...please."

He held her gaze, easing forward. "Whose ass is this?"

She thrust her breasts into the air and moaned.

Her reaction to his words shocked her. Why did she *like* the dominant way he claimed ownership of her? She'd never gloried in being owned by any male. Yet his possessiveness tweaked her. For the first time, she felt desirable, not as just an owned body, but as Lily, the female locked in Rok's violet gaze.

He pushed the head of his cock past her entrance, providing slight relief. She curled her fingers into the fabric of the platform and let her eyes roll back in her head.

"Look at me, Lily." The growl made her lids jerk back open.

"I can't," she moaned, but forced her eyes to remain wide while he slid in and out of her ass. "Too much," she whimpered.

"No, it's not. You're taking it. Taking it like a good slave." The raspy, broken quality of Rok's voice signalled his impending loss of control.

A foreign surge of female pride at being the cause of that loss of control rolled through her.

"Touch yourself," he growled.

She obeyed, threading her fingers between her legs and rubbing her clit as he'd shown her. Her cries grew more desperate, keening louder and higher with each of his thrusts.

"Whose ass is this?" he roared.

"Yours," she screamed back. "*Veck* me, Rok!"

He slammed in deep and remained there, stretching her wide and filling her ass with his hot, rainbow cum.

Her muscles were unable to clench around Rok's enormous girth, it felt as if a climax went through her, nonetheless.

Mercifully, he eased out. "Don't move," he murmured and left the sleeping platform, and then the chamber.

She couldn't have, if she'd tried. The chamber spun as she lay on her back and let the aftershocks of his plunder roll through her.

Rok returned with a damp cloth, which, unbelievably, he used to clean her. She bit her lip to keep it from quivering, hating these tears that seemed to leak each time after he forced her surrender.

Because she liked it too much. Liked the tenderness of his touch and the softness of his gaze now. The solid strength he provided when he pulled her onto his lap and held her against his chest.

She couldn't get used to it. Rok wasn't a real master—he planned to turn her in for the warrant. She wanted to ask him what it would take to convince him to keep her, but she was too afraid of his answer. She didn't think she could bear to hear him say his plans out loud.

Especially not now—after what they'd just done.

She feared she wouldn't survive it.

5

Rok maneuvered the ship onto a small landing platform on a trading outpost. He'd have given anything to just stay in space, enjoying his little human, who surrendered more to him with each passing planet rotation.

But their ship couldn't withstand the flight without repairs. He flicked off the engines, unbuckled his harness, and swiveled to survey his little prisoner. He hated to lock her up, but he also didn't have proper clothing for her.

"I'm coming with you," she said instantly, as if guessing his thoughts.

He smiled. He liked when she showed her real self—not the slave personae she'd perfected. "Mierna, do you have any pants Lily might squeeze into?" The Venusian was short, but rounder around the middle from her excessive drinking. Pants of hers just might fit his long-legged human in the waist, though they'd be too short.

Mierna muttered something and beckoned Lily to go with her. Lily flashed a grateful smile his way, which made him feel all kinds of warm. He hadn't considered taking a mate again. Not after Taraw's death. But now the thought of ever being apart from Lily rankled him. He wasn't even sure he'd be able to give her over to her mother and sister.

He waited for Lily to emerge. The pants came down to her knees, and were a close fit, molding to the shape of her ass and thighs in the most delicious way. He couldn't wait to tear them off her later. He held out his hand and took her palm, tugging her off the ship and onto the arid, desolate station. Beings of all species wove through the station, chattering in hundreds of different languages. His crew flanked him, hands at their weapons, ready for trouble.

There was no reason to expect trouble, but this was wild, ungoverned territory, which meant anything could happen.

He made inquiries about getting replacement scrap to mend the outer hull of his ship, and they were led to toothless being of an unknown species.

"Five hundred stein," the turtle-like creature demanded.

He shook his head. "Fifteen."

The turtle shrugged his shoulders and turned away.

Rok, too, went silent, waiting. In his experience, persistence often won the wrangle.

Turtle turned back. "Give me the female."

Lily shrank against his side and he immediately cursed himself for bringing her. She was far too beautiful to be safe in a wild place like this.

He took a risk and pulled a dagger, lunging forward, stopping with the tip just a millimeter from Turtle's throat. "Don't look at her," he growled. Beings around them stopped their conversations to stare. Many reached for weapons far more deadly than a blade.

The Turtle showed no sign of fear. He stared at Rok for several moments with watery eyes and then shoved his wrist and the weapon away. "Fifty."

Rok sheathed the blade. "Done."

Half a planet rotation later, they had a stack of the material outside their craft. Gaurdo and Janu argued over the best way to patch the hole while he ignored them and went to work. He'd love to have the job finished before nightfall. He had no desire to spend more time at the trading station than necessary.

The ship docked near them took off and he threw an arm over his eyes to keep out the flying grit. His protective instincts kicking into gear, he looked around for Lily.

Where had she gone?

"Lily?" he turned in a circle. She'd been hanging around behind him a short while ago. He jogged onto the ship. "Lily?" Maybe she'd gone to the washroom?

But no, he didn't find her there, nor anywhere on the ship. His heart picked up speed. Back outside the ship, he called her name, "Lily?"

Gaurdo, Jano, Jaso and Depri stopped what they were doing to look around.

"Where in the *veck* is Mierna?" Lily must be with her.

But Mierna came walking calmly toward them, a pouch of brew clutched in her little hand. "She's gone." Mierna waved a hand in the direction of the ship that had just taken off. For once she didn't appear serene when imparting information that others didn't know.

"What in the *veck* do you mean?"

Mierna pointed again. "She's been taken—she's in great danger. We must follow, before it's too late."

Vecking excrement!

He threw the material haphazardly over the hole, welding it with a ray gun. He didn't care if they had to repair it at the next stop, he just needed to get them in the air. Before he lost the first bright spot he'd had in his life in ages. Maybe ever.

~.~

LILY LAY ON THE FLOOR, hands bound behind her back, ankles trussed together and attached to her wrists. The serpent bite on her ankle throbbed in time with her heartbeat. It had taken a turn for the worse that planet rotation and now she began to feel the poison flowing through her veins. Her head ached and lips felt cracked and dry. A fever made her alternatively hot and cold.

This was it. Her life was over.

She'd made the mistake of wandering over to the ship beside them to inquire which direction they were headed. She thought she might stow away on their ship if they were going in the opposite direction as Rok.

The moment the lizard-like beings saw her, though, they'd gone crazy, chattering in a language she didn't understand. Within seconds, they'd surrounded her and one of them shot her with a stun gun. She'd woken in this storeroom closet, tied on the filthy floor.

Veck. She should have stayed with Rok. He wouldn't have really turned her in. He didn't have it in him to send her to her death. Not with the way he cared for her. She should have had the courage to ask him what his intentions were, or if they'd changed.

Instead, she'd walked into this. Whatever it was.

She was probably speeding on her way to the Ocretion authorities right now. Or perhaps to be sold as a slave to yet another master. Of course, she may die before they even arrived, because she needed medical care for her ankle wound.

She thought of Rok and wondered what he would think. Would he know where she'd gone? He'd probably believe she ran away. He probably wouldn't try to look for her.

Even so, she clung to the tiniest sliver of hope—something she shouldn't allow herself. Rok might come for her. Somehow, he might deduce which ship she'd left on and he might follow.

Please, sweet mother earth, please.

Things felt incomplete. She wasn't supposed to die this way—to leave Rok in the way she had. She needed to see him again. All her life she'd been searching for meaning. She'd thought it was about escaping, about setting up a free human colony. Now, she thought it might be much simpler than that. Maybe the meaning in life was just love. Connecting with another being. Sharing oneself. Trusting.

She coughed against the dust filling her nostrils and lungs. Love. She'd almost had it.

~.~

Rok managed to catch the ship with Lily on it. He attempted communications with it, but either it didn't have the same channels or they deliberately chose to ignore his messages. Though he wanted nothing more than to shoot their *vecking* ship out of space, that wouldn't help him get Lily back. He chose to follow at a distance, locking all tracking on their ship.

The moment it landed, he'd *vecking* storm the craft and incinerate every last one of them until he found Lily.

Mierna stared out into the space in front of them, her lips pinched. "You failed her," she declared.

His fingers curled into fists, horns stiffened with anger, even though he'd been thinking the same thing. "What in the *veck* do you mean?"

"You let her believe she might come to harm. She was looking for other options when they took her."

Ice flooded his veins. He clenched his teeth, his vision spinning. "No."

"No? Did she not think you would turn her over her masters?"

"Yes," he snarled. "But I—"

"She is ill, also. Poisoned. She may not last another planet rotation."

"She will last," he gritted. She had to. He wasn't going to lose another female he loved. Especially not this one. Lily was his mate.

He knew that now. His body had known it the moment he'd first seen her, it just had taken his mind a while to catch up. He'd never felt this way for any being before—so in need of her that taking his next breath without knowing she'd make it seemed an impossibility.

Yet he did breathe. One inhale, one exhale. Again and again as they zoomed through space.

They landed at an air station in the far outskirts of Ocretion territory. Rok docked beside them and went tearing out of the ship, weapon in hand, only to find an enormous troop of Ocretion soldiers crowded around Lily's ship.

"Lily," he shouted when he caught sight of the soldiers leading her out, wrists bound behind her back, head hanging forward. Her hair looked limp and dirty.

She looked up at his cry and what he saw terrified him. Her face was pale and sweaty, deep hollows darkened her under eyes and her lips were cracked and bleeding.

Janu and Jaso yanked him backward, into their ship when the soldiers turned and pointed toward him.

"Shut the *veck* up," Janu hissed. "Do you want them to come and arrest you, too? How will you help her then?"

He fought them, not because he believed they were wrong, but because it felt good to fight. He needed to rip someone to shreds. Gaurdo and Depri joined the tussle and he continued to fight until the four of them had him pinned to the ground, panting and cursing them like a crazed animal.

"Think. Think," Depri shouted at him. "Think your way out of this. How can you help her? Who can help?"

Who.

His body went slack. "Get off me."

They must have seen the return of reason, because his friends helped him to his feet. "We need to see Prince Zander. He has battleships and he wants Lily, too."

6

Lily sat on the hard plastic bench, shoulder to shoulder with other prisoners in the death pod. Her head still pounded, but one of the soldiers had taken pity on her and run a medical scanner over her bite wound, then delivered the antivenom.

No one knew how long they had to live. The Ocretians kept the death pods largely a secret and obviously, those who went in, never came out. It seemed they were still filling it, though. Prisoners had been filing in for three planet rotations.

Crazy though it was, she felt certain Rok was working to get her out. He'd been there when they took her. She'd heard his anguished shout, seen his friends wrestle him back in their ship. He did care about her—she knew it!

That thought alone kept her from sinking into the darkest despair. Rok had to get her out, because they belonged together, somehow. She didn't know how, nor did she care. Even if he wanted nothing more than to keep her as his sex slave for his entertainment on his flights, she'd be on board. But he'd already been willing to teach her to fly. Perhaps she'd find some use other than sex. She could be one of the crew—have a family of sorts for the first time, ever.

A human mother and child were led into the pod. The guards split the two, putting the child in Lily's cell and taking the mother away.

"No!" the woman screamed. The walls echoed with the ripping pain in her voice. "Carmeela! Give me my baby back!"

Something scraped at the back of Lily's memory—her own mother's cries. Someone had screamed for her like that. Someone had screamed herself hoarse while Lily had been carried away, kicking and crying from some kind of factory housing.

There'd been another, too. A man had tried to block them, had reached for her as she screamed his name, but he'd been stunned.

Tears burned behind her eyes. She had been loved, once.

The little girl, who couldn't be more than six sun cycles appeared in shock. She didn't cry—perhaps she'd already had that response beaten from her.

"Hey," Lily said softly. "It's going to be all right."

The girl stared at her, brown eyes wide. Her dark hair fell across her face in matted clumps, her skin was too pale. "You can sit over here, with me," she offered, though there was no room left on any of the benches.

The girl ignored her offer, though, and sat down on the floor, cross-legged. She began to rock, silently mouthing something.

"That just isn't right," the being beside her muttered. "Separating them like that. Why not let them die together?"

Lily lifted her chin. "We're not dying," she said firmly. She didn't know what made her say it, except it seemed important to keep that child from floating off, the way Lily had learned to. She didn't want her to stop living until her body died. And she sure as hell didn't want that body to die any time soon.

The old human male on her left snorted.

"It's true. We're all going to get out of here, and we're going to live on planet free of slavery. Things will grow there—beautiful plants and flowers. And the light will come down in rainbows."

The little girl lifted her head and stared at her.

She nodded, emphatically. "Everyone will be free there. No slaves.

Different species will live in harmony, with a fair government that never puts being to death. The worst punishment will be exile, and no one will ever want to earn that punishment because it's so wonderful there."

"People will sing," a cracked voice spoke from the corner.

Lily peered around to see an old Stornigian. The reminder of Janu and Jaso squeezed her chest, but she smiled encouragingly. The female cleared her throat. "Music will be everywhere. Songs and instruments. And dancing."

"There will be enough food for everyone. Delicious food they grow right there," another being chimed in.

The little girl listened, eyes round, expression rapt.

"Are you hungry, girl-child?" Another being produced a bit of a nutrition bar and offered it.

The girl looked at it warily, then glanced at Lily, as if for permission. Lily nodded and Carmeela took it, unwrapping it with grubby fingers.

"There will be water. Enough water to sink your body into. And colors. Every kind of color you've ever seen, everywhere," a middle-aged human female offered. "And art. Artists from all over the galaxy will go there to create beautiful works."

The child spoke for the first time. "What is art?"

The woman smiled. "Art is when you make something you love, just because it's beautiful. Just because you want to."

"Why?"

"For others to enjoy. Or for your own enjoyment. It could be something you look at, or listen to, or watch."

"I made a house, once, out of mud," the child said. "They said it was forbidden."

"You see?" The woman sounded triumphant. "On the planet we're going to, it will never be forbidden. You can make whatever you like."

"Will my mother be there?"

"Yes," Lily said immediately. "Your mother will certainly be there."

She held her breath to keep the tears from choking her throat. It had to be true—every promise they'd made. It just had to be true. She would give anything to make it true.

~.~

Rok and his crew disembarked onto the landing dock of Zander's palatial pod. He had requested permission to land on the basis of having urgent news about Lily, the sister of prince's mate.

The Zandian guards met them and bowed as if they were honored guests. He hid his surprise and returned the bow, following the males briskly through the halls to the Great Room, where Zander sat on a raised dais. He wore a white tunic and pants, made of a finely woven material that probably cost more than twice Rok's ship. A ceremonial sword hung at his waist. The prince's copper-haired mate and her mother stood nearby, and the four male advisors from his previous visit flanked him, also dressed in white.

He bowed to the prince and went straight to the *vecking* point. "I had her and I lost her. She's on an Ocretion death pod. I need your help to get her free."

Zander surged to his feet and stepped down from the dais, responding to the urgency in Rok's tone. "What death pod? Where?"

"Outer limits of the territory."

One of the advisors, the huge, battle-scarred warrior named Seke, moved closer to Lily's mother, Leora. in what appeared to be a protective stance. The woman, whose beauty shone as bright as her daughters', had gone pale and she clutched the back of Zander's unoccupied throne with white knuckles.

Zander addressed one of his advisors. "Daneth, contact the authorities and attempt to purchase her. Tell them I will pay any amount."

Daneth bowed. "I will do my best, my lord." He swiftly exited.

Zander paced a few feet, then stopped and rubbed his face. "Tell me."

"She was on Jesel, captive of other humans there. I bought her." *And tortured her.* Pain seared his chest. He had mistreated her. After everything she'd been through, he'd used her a sex slave, had caused her to suffer in the belief she was on her way to her death.

Lamira's green gaze locked on him, and he felt certain she read his thoughts, knew his sins. "She knows you're coming for her," she murmured.

A shudder ran through his body.

If ever he believed in a *vecking* destiny, he knew this was his. He *would* rescue Lily. It was an impossible task, but he would do anything and everything he could to get her out of there. She was his destiny.

"I wish to use some of your battle ships." He'd never been one to pussy foot around.

Zander folded his arms across his chest, mistrust evident in his gaze. "What is your plan?"

He didn't have a *vecking* clue. "All six of us can fly." He indicated himself and his crew. "We'll attack and force the death pod out of territory. There's a unincorporated planet not far from there. If we can get them to land, then I'll storm the pod and rescue Lily."

"That will never work."

He glaced at Lamira, hoping she'd entreat her mate, but she remained silent, breath held, watching them both.

Zander, too, looked at Lamira. She didn't move, didn't blink, but her wide green eyes pleaded.

With a frustrated gesture, Zander turned to one of the guards. "Show them to guest quarters." To Rok, he said, "We'll see what Daneth finds out from the Ocretion government. Then we'll talk."

Rok wanted to smash the colorful walls of the well-appointed palace. He didn't have time to wait. Lily was speeding to her death, as they stood there. But what else could he do? Gnashing his teeth, he stalked out behind the guard, knowing courtesy demanded he bow first but not giving a *veck*.

"Rok," Zander called him back.

He stiffened.

"The crystal bath will be made available to you if you need it."

This time he forced a stiff bow, though he couldn't bring himself to thank the male. His body did crave the crystal light, though. Just being in the palatial pod, where the crystals were embedded in every skylight, made his body hum with energy and vitality.

He made his way straight to the crystal bath, stripped his clothes off and laid down on one of the beds, absorbing the rainbow light. He closed his eyes, allowing the color to permeate his skin, to recharge his life force. He wanted Lily to see this room. Though before, he'd hated that he had to come here, seen his need for the light recharge a weakness, now he imagined it through her eyes. She would find it beautiful. He would feed her chocolate and while she lay in a bed beside him and... What?

What was this ridiculous future he was imagining? Did he think he'd be living here at the palatial pod with Lily and her family? As if Zander would have him—a smuggler with three warrants out for his arrest and a rag tag scrappy crew.

And yet, he knew for certain that if—no, *when*—he got Lily back, he would never want to let her leave his side again.

Veck.

~.~

LAMIRA WATCHED Zander pace the length of the Great Hall, his muscular shoulders tensed into hard knots. The rest of the gathering had exited, leaving them alone in the lavish hall. Her plants grew in pots all around the room—banana plants, tomatoes, peppers, fig trees. So many incredible rare varieties of Earth-based food bearing plants, grown from heirloom seeds. She would plant these on Zandia, when they recovered the planet.

Zander stopped and scrubbed a hand across his jaw. She knew his affection for her was clashing with his singular purpose in life—to take back Zandia. Giving up six airships to a probable death mission would not only hurt his chances, but if his involvement was linked to it, would endanger his position as a recognized ambassador and his chances of mounting an army against the Finn—the species who had taken over Zandia when he was a boy.

"Lamira, you know I want to help—" he began.

She stiffened, sensing the *but* that was sure to follow.

He stopped speaking, regret washing over his face, probably at her expression. He had not always been so in tune with her emotions. When he'd first purchased her for breeding, his inability to decipher her human complexities angered him and resulted in many misunderstandings. But he was learning. He blew out his breath.

"Tell me, have you foreseen this? Any of it?"

She sucked on her lower lip, debating what to say. She had once hidden her claircognizance from him, but now believed she was destined to use it to aid in his purpose—regaining Zandia.

She, too, saw danger, even death facing the warrior Rok and his mission. But if he had Zander's full crew as part of the mission...well, she didn't see the outcome, but the energy felt enormous. Powerful. As if great things might happen.

But it would be hard enough to convince Zander to give Rok six ships. For him to throw in his own life, and the lives of his best warriors, as well, would be an impossibility. Especially when this was not his battle.

She dropped a hand to her abdomen, sensing their baby's peaceful energy. Could she gamble that little life in order to save her sister's?

The baby seemed to agree.

"Rok will be successful," she said. It was not a lie. A misdirection, perhaps, but not a lie. He would be successful if everything fell into place. But in order for that to happen, she would have to force Zander into action.

7

Rok slipped into the pilot's seat of Zander's gleaming state-of-the art battleship and his cock nearly grew hard at the power he felt.

How he had convinced Zander to let them take the crafts, he still wasn't sure. He had a feeling the prince's little human mate had a lot to do with it. After his luxurious crystal light bath, and Mierna's disastrous one—she had asked to try it out and had become violently ill, throwing up for the rest of the planet rotation—Zander had informed them that Daneth's request had been denied and he would grant them four ships. Rok had argued again for six, but Zander held firm. Clearly he thought they wouldn't return.

Veck him.

Rok had a date with his *vecking* destiny and her name was Lily. He fired up the engine, closing his eyes to savor the ferocious purr. He flicked all the switches on, adjusted the controls and eased out of Zander's hanger. Touching the control on his collar, he established communications with Gaurdo, Depri and Mierna, his other pilots. Janu and Jaso had split to ride with Depri and Gaurdo, respectively.

He eased out into the dense traffic surrounding the capitol, keeping it slow so his friends could follow. Gradually, they fought their way up, into clearer air space, and eventually, he punched the speed and they exited the planet's atmosphere in the direction of the death pod. He started to switch over to autopilot, when a beep sounded over the ship's controls.

"Rok, this is Zander." The prince's clipped tones came through.

He rolled his eyes, wondering what warning the prince had for him. "Yes, my lord?"

Silence ensued, then Zander snapped, *"Where is my vecking mate?"*

A door swishing open behind him made him groan. *Vecking* stars, did stowing away run in the family?

He leaned forward. "I *vecking* swear I didn't know she was on the ship. I did not take your mate."

"Confirm now. You do or do not have my mate on board that ship?" The panic he heard in the prince's voice made him wince.

"I do have her," he groaned. "But I didn't invite her."

"What about her mother."

He hadn't made eye contact with Lamira yet, but he did now, brows raised. The pretty human stood framed in the doorway, her mother behind her.

"Yes, her too."

"Turn the ship around and return, immediately."

He ground his teeth. Zander might be able to disable the ship from afar. He also was likely to kill him for kidnapping his mate. And Lily's life was hanging on the line.

"Negative, my lord. My mission is still intact. I will return after I have reunited your mate with her sister."

Zander's curses and the sound of something smashing came across the speakers. "You *vecking* get back here now or I will cut off your *vecking* cock and shove it down your throat. My mate is with child, do you understand me?"

Veeeeck. He should have guessed by the full breasts and slight rounding at her belly.

He started flipping controls to cut off the prince, but the male's curses and threats still came through. Finally he found the right switch and the board went silent.

He slumped back in his seat, ignoring his uninvited guests.

"He will follow. Give him time to catch up, you'll need all the ships you can get to attack the death pod."

Shock shot up his expression, raising his brows right to horn level. "You planned this? To get him involved?"

She slid into the seat beside him, her palms pressed over her abdomen protectively. "It was the only way."

"What *are* you?"

Leora drifted in and settled in the seat behind them.

"I have gifts similar to those of a Venusian. The Zandian crystals enhanced them, which may be why Mierna grew sick from them."

"It probably sent her into a detox," he muttered. "You do realize Zander is going to kill me now?"

"He won't kill you. Zandians are on the brink of extinction—all Zandian lives are important to him."

He didn't want to ask the next question but curiosity got the better of him. "So what does he do with criminals?"

"He has a dungeon in the pod. He keeps them there." She spoke lightly, as if his fate to spend the rest of his life in a pod dungeon wasn't worrisome.

He touched the communications device at his collar. Zander probably had access to this frequency, but he didn't mind. "We're going to modify speed until the prince and his fleet join us."

"Copy that," they each replied.

He flipped the switch enjoining him to Zander's communications back on. "Waiting for your arrival, my lord. Do you need our coordinates?"

"I don't need your *vecking* coordinates," Zander growled over the lines. It sounded as if his teeth were clenched. "Estimated arrival, 1600."

"Copy that."

~.~

Singing.

The entire death pod was filled with singing. Beautiful, mournful songs.

The guards had attempted to stop it at first, shocking the woman in Lily's cell who began it, but then others picked it up where she left off and their leader had shrugged and said, "there's no harm in it. Let them sing. It's better than wailing."

Now, voices joined together in song after song. They came in different languages, repeated until everyone learned the words. Chants, songs, spirituals. Suppressed religious songs. She'd never heard any of them before, but the effect on her was enormous. The voices carried her away. Not in the absent-from-body way she'd refined, but in a sort of euphoria. Joy. Solidarity. Communion. Peace.

Rok would come for her. She knew it in her bones. Just like she'd always known her life had more meaning than a colorless sex slave. He was her *after*. The life she hadn't yet begun. The promised land she'd described to the sweet child now sleeping in her lap.

Rok would come and they all would be free.

~.~

Their ten cloaked battleships surrounded the death pod. Rok sent out a communications jammer to interrupt any signals they might be sending or receiving. He didn't need them calling for help or identifying the battleships.

"Fire without incurring damage. We don't want to cause any explosions or even disable the ship, only to force it out of territory," Rok barked over the communications. "On my count, one...two...three, and *fire*."

Laser fire blasted and the huge death pod rocked. It lacked the ability to fly quickly or nimbly, so it simply made a slow bank to the left.

Good. Exactly the direction they wanted it to turn.

"Keep the pressure on the right, keep it turning!"

Beside him, Lamira was strapped in, hands gripping the control panel. She'd gone pale. "I think I'm going to be sick."

"*Vecking* excrement—do it that way." He pointed to her other side.

Leora rubbed her back and offered a container of fluid.

"Now, stay right on it! Oh *veck*."

Smoke issued from one of the pod's turning vents and it wobbled and spun in a circle.

"Push it back, push it back toward the land mass." He prayed the pilot of the death pod was good enough to get control of the thing and land safely.

But the giant death pod began to plunge, spinning out of control through the atmosphere of the land mass melow.

"Send out magnerays to stabilize it!" He sent his battleship into a dive after the pod.

Veck, he had no idea if their ships had enough power to stabilize the thing, even with them all working simultaneously.

He aimed and shot the magneray, which struck the pod and interrupted the spinning. It still wobbled horribly, but—- There. Depri's magneray caught the pod from the opposite side, providing more stability. One by one, the other battleships sent out magnerays which attached, until together they held the pod stable and aloft.

"Lower her down slowly," he barked, easing his own craft toward land.

The ships worked together, bringing the pod down by degrees, tipping and tilting it as they went. Sweat dripped down Rok's brow. It took every bit of his concentration to maintain contact with the pod and keep the thing from crashing to the land mass below.

"That's it...keep going. Easy now...Whoa!" The far side of the pod dropped when three ships lost contact with it, but Prince Zander swooped down below and sent a beam upward to catch them and steady the fall. "Good work, my lord."

They continued to descend, meter by meter. An alarm went off, warning his engine was too hot from the exertion of the magneray. "Almost there," he muttered, trying to turn the *vecking* sound off.

"Move out of the way, your highness or you'll be crushed," he barked as they got close to the ground. He shifted his ship around to another side to help stabilize the side Zander would drop. "On three. One...two...three!"

Zander moved out and the pod dipped sharply. The alarm screeched, lights flashed, but they got the thing to the ground. Smoke issued from every side of it.

He brought his ship to land beside it.

"Outside atmosphere is unsafe for breathing," spoke a robotic female voice of his ship. He wasn't surprised, otherwise the land mass would be inhabited, but it made things difficult, especially with the smoke issuing from the Death Pod. The passengers would need fresh air to breathe, and soon.

"My crew—board with arms drawn. Prepare to fight. Depri, destroy all tracking devices on the pod."

Zander issued a similar order to his men.

He unbuckled his harness and pressed ray guns into each of the women's hands. "You two stay here. Do not unlock the door for anyone but myself or Zander. Understand?"

Lamira nodded, but he wasn't sure he trusted her. "I mean it. If anything happens to you, it's on my head."

She rested her hand on her belly. "Nothing will happen to me."

With a curse, he fastened a helmet with controlled air delivery over his head, left the ship and sealed the door, sprinting to the entrance of the death pod, which Depri already had burned half way open with a laser ray.

~.~

The moment the death pod had been impacted, she knew Rok had come for her. Now that they'd landed, smoke filled the corridors in thick plumes, making it impossible to see even a hand in front of her face.

She scooped Carmeela into her arms and cradled her against her hip, holding her tight, as if that might somehow protect her from suffocation. Far away, she heard the muffled sound of Rok shouting her name.

"Rok!" she screamed, but choked on smoke, coughing and wheezing. "Rok…Rok! I'm here!"

"Rok!" one of the males in her cell shouted.

"Rok!" Another one cried. Someone thumped the heel of his shoe against the wall to make a thump. "Rok! Rok! Rok!" More voices joined, creating a chant of his name.

Tears moistened her eyes. They were doing this for her. Well, her rescue might free all of them, but they were working together. It never happened. Ocretions kept lower caste beings from organizing, developing relationships. They forced separation, but in this moment, they all cried out as one. "Rok! Rok! Rok!"

A door burst open at the end of the corridor. Every cell door slid open.

"*Lily!*" Rok's deep voice rang with urgency.

Hands justled her and Carmeela forward, thrusting her in the direction of Rok. "She's here!" someone yelled. "Right here."

Through the black haze, Rok's hulking figure appeared. His face set with ferocious intent, he appeared like a demon. No, like a god.

"Rok!" she shrieked and threw herself at him, Carmeela still in her arms.

Momentary surprise registered on his face at the child, but he promptly wrapped them both up in an embrace, his arms like steel bands around her, lifting them off the ground and swiftly carrying her back out the door.

"You came for me."

"Of course I came for you," he said gruffly. "You belong to me."

The sensation those words produced was all warmth. It wasn't the twisted knife in the chest that came with being considered an object for trade and use, but the soaring joy of *belonging*. What she'd longed for from the moment she met Rok—to be a part of his circle, his crew, his life. Being owned by Rok carried an entirely different meaning than slavery to her, and she knew it did to him, too.

"Every being follow me. Remain calm and orderly. Help those who are having difficulty," Rok's loud voice echoed off the corridor walls as he swept forward. They entered a large antechamber with less smoke.

"Every being get down on the floor, where the air is most clear," Rok ordered. He immediately unclipped his helmet and reached to put it on her, but she deflected it and put it over Carmeela's little head instead.

"We have to find her mother," she said urgently.

Two males of the same species as Rok strode in, swords in their hands, appearing as fierce and deadly as Rok.

She gaped.

The younger one gave her an assessing sweep. "You have found Lily."

She started at his use of her name. Was this Rok's brother? No, he'd been orphaned and taken in by Janu and Jaso. Who, then were these males?

"Where is my mate?" the handsome Zandian demanded.

"On my ship. Is the pod secure?"

Lily blinked, utterly confused.

"Yes," the older Zandian answered.

"Let's go together, then." Rok hooked an arm around her waist just as Carmeela's mother screamed her name from across the room.

Lily started toward her and Rok instantly followed, providing protection as she moved through the crowded chamber.

"Carmeela!" the mother screamed again.

"It's all right," Lily shouted. "She's safe."

Rok shouldered through the crowd, delivering them to the weeping mother.

"Oh thank you, thank the stars." The mother claimed her little girl, hugging her tightly against her chest.

Before she could answer, Rok tugged her back through the crowd, his broad shoulders and extra height making it easy for him to cut through. In this setting, it hit her full force what a magnificent specimen of male warrior he was—solid muscle, radiating strength and confident capability.

He'd come for her. She hadn't been wrong about his feelings for her. Something beautiful took flight in her chest and the tears burning her eyes weren't only from the smoke.

The other two Zandian warriors waited near the door and Rok steered her in their direction. "Come on, beautiful. There's several beings you will want to meet."

~.~

ROK'S HAND trembled on the hilt of his sword. The death pod had been packed with beings—perhaps 600 in all, with the cells set up as waste receptacles--designed to open at the floor to dump all the prisoners into outer space. No wonder they'd flown to the outer region of the galaxy. Stars, if he'd been even a minute late, he would have lost Lily forever.

His Lily.

Lily had not been a helpless victim, she'd led the group. Somehow she'd won the support of everyone in her cell, and taken on the welfare of a small child. By the one true Zandian star, he loved this female.

He kept her close as they traversed through the corridors, which were gradually clearing of smoke as the pod's oxygen systems circulated and cleaned the air. He put his helmet over Lily's head and grabbed one from a dead guard for himself to protect them on the short trip to the battleship. Zander followed closely behind, asking Seke to stay behind to keep the peace, if necessary.

His heart thudded in his chest as they traversed the rocky terrain. Guilt over keeping Lamira and Leora's existence from Lily twisted like a knot in his solar plexus.

He wished he had a moment with her alone to prepare her, but things were never easy.

He activated the hatch and they entered. Lamira launched herself at Zander. Although the prince clutched her tightly, his face remained as if made of stone.

Leora's attention was only for Lily, though. She stepped forward, tears glinting in her eyes. "Lily?" she rasped.

Rok cleared his throat. His poor female appeared lost, brow furrowed, shoulders tense. "I should have told you," he said immediately, before she could say it, herself. Of course she still didn't know what in the *veck* was happening.

"Forgive me, Lily. I knew you had family searching for you. I was selfish. I wanted to surprise you."

"Surprise me?" she repeated blankly, looking from Leora to Lamira. She surely must recognize her own features in their faces.

"Your mother, Leora. And a younger sister, Lamira, mate to Zander, exiled prince of Zandia."

Lily's knees buckled and he snapped her up against his side to keep her from falling.

"I understand it's a shock. And I know if I would've told you, you might not have tried to escape me. I will forever bear the guilt of losing you."

"Mother?" Lily whispered, confusion still etched on her face.

"And sister."

Lamira stepped forward beside her mother, after casting a worried glance at Zander.

Leora's eyes shone with tears. "I feared we'd never find you," she choked and opened her arms.

A bewildered Lily stepped into them, but didn't return the

embrace. When Leora released her, Lamira stepped forward, but Lily only accepted a cursory embrace before turning back and staring up at him.

"You knew?" she rasped.

He tried to swallow, but the knot in his throat made it impossible. "Forgive me, Lily. I met them before I bought you on Jesel."

"So...so you never intended to turn me over to the Ocretions?"

Regret stabbed him. "I shouldn't have let you think that."

To his shock, a slow smile spread across her face and then a manic laugh bubbled out of her. "You were going to surprise me?" She threw her arms around his neck, jumping to reach. He caught her under her seat and boosted her legs around his waist.

"You're not mad?"

"You *did* intend to keep me." Triumph and joy bubbled up with more laughter.

"You're mine," he said gruffly into her neck.

A few tears dripped down Lily's face, but she was still laughing. Lamira and Leora wore faint, curious smiles.

Zander cleared his throat. "You are welcome on my pod with your mother and sister, Lily."

It was everything he could do to keep from growling *"Mine!"* at the prince.

Lily twisted and he reluctantly placed her on the ground, turning her around so her back pressed against his front with his arms wrapped around her. "What will happen to the other prisoners? They can't go back to Ocretia. Where will they go?"

When Zander's expression showed nothing, she turned pleading eyes on him.

She wanted his help. Trusted him to solve her problem. She believed in him. His heart swelled too big for his chest. He suddenly owned his destiny—the complete one that Mierna had always predicted. The one Lamira, too, had promised.

Your destiny is woven with ours. You were born to lead armies.

Rok cleared his throat. "I will train them as soldiers and pilots. They can help us take back Zandia."

A tiny jerk of Zander's head showed his surprise.

Lamira's face broke into a broad smile. "I knew you would be the one."

But Lily frowned. "And what then? They will be slaves of Zandia?"

Zander stiffened. "Zandians do not keep slaves."

Both Rok and Lily's eyes traveled to Lamira's collar, but they kept their mouths shut. She was obviously far more than a slave to Zander, whatever their situation may be.

"Any human who fights for Zandia will be considered a full and free citizen," Zander declared, though it appeared to cost him.

The three lovely humans rewarded Zander with brilliant smiles. "Thank you, my lord," Lamira murmured.

"We can remain in the death pod, so long as you provide us with supplies. Training can begin immediately." He cleared his throat, hating—despising—what he had to offer next. "Lily, if you want to go with your family—"

"I'll stay and train with you," she cut in immediately and something akin to fireworks exploded in his body, warming him, sending sparks of happiness showering everywhere. He squeezed her so tight she had to slap his arms so she could breathe.

This was it—his destiny. He knew because Lily was at his side.

Purpose and direction had never been clearer. Achieving a goal never easier.

"My lord, I have one personal request."

Zander arched a brow. "Yes?"

His throat tightened. "I wish to mark my mate with a Zandian crystal, as is our ancient tradition."

Zander's expression softened and he glanced at his own mate with the same fierce need Rok felt every time he was near Lily. "Of course, Rok. I will send it with the first supplies."

Lily twisted in his arms to gaze up at him. "Am I your mate?"

He brushed her coppery hair from her face. 'Yes, pet. You're mine. Only mine. Always mine. Forever mine." He cupped her chin. "Any arguments?"

She shook her head and whispered, "No."

8

Rok escorted Lily into one the guard's sleeping chamber that he'd selected as their own. They'd spent the most of the planet rotation convincing the humans that Zandia was the promised land, and all they needed to do to earn their freedom was to help win it for Zander. Though doubt lingered in the air, it wasn't as if they had any other options or choices. Lily just hoped after they received fair treatment, they would come to believe.

"You have to the count of five to get those clothes off," Rok growled, his eyes glowing deep violet with desire.

Her gaze flicked to his stiffened horns, then dropped lower to the considerable bulge in his flight pants. He'd been sending her hungry looks all planet rotation, along with keeping her pinned to his side at all times as if he feared she might be taken from him again.

Prince Zander and left with her mother and sister, who had promised to send her clothing and supplies.

She shimmied out of her filthy slave dress and Mierna's flight pants. Her nipples pebbled up in the cool air, pussy clenched under Rok's lustful stare. "I really should get cleaned up," she murmured.

Rok groaned and his huge hands palmed her ass and lifting her to straddle his waist. "Can't wait...." He nipped her neck, licked up the column of her neck to suck on her earlobe.

Her bare core rested against his hardened cock and she rocked her hips, trying to rub her clit against the fabric of his flight pants.

"You want this cock, Lily?"

"Yes," she moaned.

"You're going to get it. You're going to get it so hard and so long your eyeballs will flip backward in your head. And then you'll get it some more. I'm going pound that little pussy until you understand this is the last cock you'll ever take. Understand me?"

A wave of heat washed over her at the possessiveness he showed. Each time he asserted his ownership of her, it healed some small part of her that feared she'd always be alone, separate.

She reached for one of his horns, but he stopped her. "You do that, pet, and your first *vecking* will be remarkably short. And I just promised you a rough ride."

She laughed and the huskiness in her voice echoed in the small chamber.

He whirled and pushed her up against the wall, shoving his pants down to free his cock. "You take this cock deep now, beautiful." He rubbed the head over her slit, testing her readiness. There was no need. Her sex dripped for him, slick and open.

Despite his harsh words, he eased into her inch by inch, giving her time to adjust to his enormous size. "You're so *vecking* tight, Lily." He withdrew a little, then thrust in and up, shoving her higher on the wall. "I will never grow tired of this beautiful little pussy."

Hooking her legs over his arms, he shoved her knees high and pinned her in place while pistoning in and out of her.

Her head lolled on the wall, eyes already rolling back as he'd promised. "Rok," she croaked in alarm, already on the brink of an orgasm.

"Go ahead, pet," he husked, still slamming in and out of her. "I'm going to keep you orgasming all night long."

Her internal muscles clamped down, squeezing and pumping his cock.

He drilled deep and held, allowing her to climax.

She reached for one of his horns and the shocked pleasure that contorted his face pushed her over the brink. She squeezed and rubbed the horn until his mouth opened on a roar and he shoved in and up five times fast, then filled her with hot streams of his luminescent cum.

She cried out, eyes closed, her senses overloaded. Sparks of light danced before her eyes.

"It'll be part of your punishment," Rok murmured, rocking slowly into her again.

Her eyes fluttered open. "What will? What punishment?" she panted, her brain unable to make sense of his words so soon after their mind-blowing sex.

His smirk was wicked. "Forced orgasms. I'm going to make you come until you cry, my little prisoner."

She came again, her internal muscles pulsing around his cock.

"What for?" Her voice cracked, though not from fear—only from spent desire and the building tension of renewed lust.

"For leaving me, pet." Rok eased away from the wall, taking her with him, still impaled on his cock. He carried her to the sleeping platform where he settled with his back against the wall. He lifted her easily by the waist and flipped her over, so she lay sprawled across his thighs. His huge hand clapped down on her upturned ass and she cried out in indignation. "It's a lesson I'm going to make sure you learn very well, Lily."

"Wait—"

But Rok continued to spank her, his paddle-like hand clapping down on first her right cheek, then left. In her post-orgasmic state, she registered the pain acutely, her nerves sizzling under the hard, continuous spanks. After more strokes than she could count, he paused and rubbed her blazing flesh, tipping her hip up to slide one hand beneath her. His middle finger slid seductively along her plump, wet folds.

"Are you sorry, Lily?" Both taunting and seduction rang in his tone.

"Yes," she warbled. "So sorry."

His finger found her clit and he rubbed the swollen nubbin, causing her to squirm with excitement. She thought she could manage the building tension until his thumb pushed against her anus.

"No," she cried, squeezing her buttocks.

He slapped the back of each thigh, making her shriek. "Naughty pet." He couldn't have sounded more loving. Affection glowed in his words. He spit on her crack and parted her cheeks with two fingers, then pushed again at her back pucker while he made a tight circle around her throbbing clitoris.

"Rok!"

His thumb penetrated into her ass.

She gasped at the sensation.

Rok worked his thick digit in and out of her ass while flicking and rubbing her clit. For a second time, explosions of sensation blinded her. The wave of pleasure send her crashing into another orgasm. She bucked, squeezing her cheeks around his hand, pussy contracting around nothing.

"Rok," she sobbed his name again.

"That's it, beautiful. I love to watch you climax." He eased his fingers out of her.

She felt as if she were soaring, her body suspended in the air, floating on the power of Rok's attention.

"Now, we'll get you cleaned up." He rolled her up into his arms and stood. "And don't think I won't *veck* you hard from behind in the shower again. Stars, I'll never forget that first *veck* for as long as I live."

"Why not?" She held her breath, dying for his answer.

He paused by the door and gazed down at her with such a fierce expression of love it made her heart stall. "Because I knew right then I'd never be able to live without you. Your little body fit with mine, like we were made for each other. Do you feel the same way, Lily?"

"Yes." She touched his scarred face. "Rok, despite the fact that I've been a sex slave for the past seven years, you're the first and only male who ever aroused me."

A satisfied smile crept over his face. "Say it again."

She giggled. "You're the only male."

"Say you belong to me—with me. You know I meant, that don't you?"

"I know," she whispered. "I belong to you. And with you. I'm yours."

"And I'm only for you," he said gruffly. "Freeing Zandia?" He shook his head. "It's for you. Not for Zander or this pod full of humans. It's what you want for them, so it's what I will do. I'm yours to command, as much as you're mine."

Tears welled in her eyes, but she blinked them back, laying her cheek against his heart. "I love you, Rok."

"Do you, beautiful? I'm not sure how that's possible, but I sure as *veck* will take it. I need you like breath. If that's love, it's what I feel."

EPILOGUE

Leora answered Zander's summons, finding him in the Great Hall, staring at one of Lamira's plants without appearing to see it. He'd been silent on the flight back to his pod and her daughter's anxiety had grown when he refused to speak with her.

Her daughter had expected punishment for putting herself into danger. Zander was quick to deliver physical correction, but judging from Lamira's blushes, they weren't entirely unenjoyable.

Lamira had been in tears that morning, saying he'd acted like a stranger, hardly acknowledging her when they returned to his chamber.

"Perhaps he needs time to think about how best to punish you," she'd suggested over breakfast.

"The last time he doubted me, he set me aside," she fretted.

"You are carrying his young. He will not set you aside," she'd promised. But looking at him now, she wasn't so sure. He still wore the withdrawn, stony expression he'd had since the previous planet rotation.

"You asked for me, my lord?"

He fingered a leaf absently. "Yes."

When he said nothing, she approached him, stopping a few feet away.

"You are my guest here, Leora."

"Yes, my lord."

"When I bought you, it was as a gift to Lamira. I have not made any demands of your service other than as her companion."

She dropped her head, sensing the rebuke that was coming. "Yes, my lord."

"As her mother, I would expect you to hold her health and well-being as the utmost priority. Even moreso because she is with child."

"Yes, my lord, that is why—"

"No," he cut her off. "Do not give me any explanation—I have no patience for your excuses. Allowing Lamira to risk her life as she did was unacceptable."

She kept her eyes trained on the floor. "Yes, my lord."

"You have displeased me, and I require that you be punished."

A knot tightened in her middle. Would Zander punish her himself? Lamira had suspected, when he'd first bought Leora, that he intended to use her, too, as a sex slave. How would she react to hearing Zander had punished her.

A movement drew her attention to the doorway. Master Seke, the warrior, stood in perfect stillness. How long had he been there?

"I have asked Master Seke to punish you."

Her belly fluttered as Seke's deep amethyst gaze held hers.

"As it seems you require a direct master and it is inappropriate for me to take that role, you will now answer to him. He will take responsibility for you and your behavior."

She couldn't seem to breathe.

"Your obedience training begins today."

PREVIEW TRAINING HIS HUMAN (ZANDIAN MASTERS BOOK 3)

Veck, no.

Seke wasn't taking on a human slave.

It had been one thing for Zander, the prince of their species, to purchase and breed the human slave, Lamira. Her genes best matched his for producing offspring. But Seke had no desire for offspring, not after the pain of losing three.

Nor did he have need for a sex slave. Or a mate.

He'd sworn celibacy when he lost Becka, his mate and the mother of his children, during the Finnian invasion of his home planet, Zandia.

But Prince Zander stood, moody and dark at the palatial pod window, ordering him to take control of Leora, Lamira's mother. The proud and beautiful female human. The one who had captivated him from the moment she arrived. At fifty solar cycles, he was still in his prime for a Zandian and his libido had not slowed, despite his vow.

She fascinated Seke with her delicate, soft features and exotic looks. Her proud demeanor more befit a queen than a slave. It showed strength of character. Power and self-control. Things he didn't expect in a female. But that didn't mean he wanted to own her or train her. To keep her in his room as his sex slave.

"I'm not a slave-keeper." He sounded stiff. It was not often—perhaps never—he and Zander crossed hairs. Though his role as Master at Arms was loyal protector, as well as director of all war strategy and security, the prince was like a son to him. He'd practically raised him since he rescued him from Zandia during the takeover. He'd saved Zander, rather than his own family—a choice he had to live with every day.

Zander usually demonstrated a deep respect for Seke, who functioned not only as a friend and mentor, but also as his Master at Arms, who'd trained him in battle arts. Now, though, he made an impatient gesture. "Nor was I, but circumstances necessitate adaptation. I believe you've told me that at least once."

Seke closed his eyes, debating whether his sense of honor would allow him to outright refuse this order. "You wish me to punish her and train her to obey me as her master?"

"Exactly so."

"Do you imagine I will breed her?" The Zandian species was nearly extinct, with no females of breeding age remaining, which was why Zander had taken a human for breeding.

Zander, at last, turned from the window and leaned back against it, folding his arms over his chest. "No. I promised Lamira when her mother arrived she would never be used that way. You will honor my word in that respect."

He ought to be relieved by that pronouncement—breaking the vow of celibacy he made in Becka's memory would be cause for quarrel. Besides, as a Master Warrior, he believed sex had the effect of scattering one's energy. Before Zander had bought Lamira, Seke had advised him not to dally with females until it was time to breed. But the fact that Leora was off limits niggled Seke, too.

"So why don't you do it? You already keep and discipline one slave, how different—"

"Punishment arouses them."

Seke's jaw went slack, visions of a humbled and aroused Leora making his cock thicken. "Pardon me?"

Zander nodded. "You understood me. Daneth inserted sensors in Lamira to aid in breeding. I discovered—"

Seke's chest had constricted and he waved a hand, not wishing to hear more. The thought of any male monitoring Leora that way—or observing her arousal during a punishment—made him clench his fists. It was an odd reaction for him—a highly trained and disciplined warrior who usually kept all emotion checked.

"So I cannot punish her, as I am mated to her daughter. It would be wrong. You seemed like the next best alternative."

"Why?" he demanded, though he already knew the answer. He'd shown a proprietary interest in Leora since the day she arrived. That didn't mean he wanted her, though.

He had no desire for a female—not for mating, nor for sex.

"Shall I ask Daneth?"

Vecking Zander! Too *vecking* observant for his own good. He knew Seke wouldn't stand for any other male touching Leora.

"No," he clipped. If the *vecking* physician so much as thought about putting monitoring devices in Leora or punishing her, he'd tear his limbs off.

Seke changed tactics. This order to train Leora wasn't about the human being unruly or undisciplined. It was about Zander's unresolved anger with his own slave-mate. The pregnant Lamira had essentially run away—leaving with her mother and the warrior Rok in pursuit of her sister, causing Zander to give chase and enter a war between humans and Ocretions that they could not afford to engage in.

"Have you punished your mate yet for leaving?" He knew Zander had not, because the prince had hardly spoken to her that morning, acting like a stranger. Both Leora and Lamira had been quiet and subdued, Lamira's sad eyes following her mate with longing.

Zander's eyes flashed dangerously purple. "That is not your concern."

Like *veck*, it wasn't. If the leader of the Zandian species allowed his personal relations to affect the way he led and the decisions he made, it was exactly Seke's concern. But he didn't say that. *Respect, honor, obedience.* He had pledged himself to Zander's father and to the crown of Zandia. He did not give of himself conditionally.

He rubbed his ear. "You wish Leora punished. And trained."

"Daneth will send the equipment to your chamber and can instruct you on its use. You will keep her there, with you, until she demonstrates complete obedience and bonding with you as her master."

Bonding. Was that why punishment aroused them? Was that how the Ocretion slave masters had enforced obedience? Punishment and breeding? Was their arousal at punishment the trait that made humans good slaves? He'd always thought it their weaker physical and over-emotional constitution. The thought made him want to kick down a wall. Who else had punished Leora? Had they used her for sex? For breeding?

But no. Both her daughters had been sired by Johan, the human revolutionary, killed during the last slave revolt. Seke relaxed by a degree. Still, the need to know each and every master who'd ever touched her, to seek those masters out and destroy them rose like a hot flame, giving him a restless, angry energy. He flexed his fingers to keep them from clenching.

So Zander expected him to punish her to arousal, *not* have sex with her, and still establish a bond. He supposed it was possible. He'd trained many males in battle arts, establishing a master-student bond. But with Leora, the female who already tempted him from his vow of celibacy on a daily basis...*veck.*

"Very well. I will do as you command. But with all due respect, I suggest you resolve matters with your own mate. Humans have delicate constitutions. Lamira appears stressed by your disregard and it could affect the young she carries."

Zander's eyes flashed and he surged forward on his feet, his chest nearly bumping Seke's. "You worry about your slave, I'll worry about mine."

Veck.

His slave. One he had to punish in the most intimate manner, who would become aroused when he did so. How in the stars would he manage?

~.~

Leora entered the Great Hall of the palatial pod, summoned there by Prince Zander. "You asked for me, my lord?"

He had called her to his opulent throne room, no doubt to inform her she had displeased him by allowing her daughter—the prince's pregnant mate—to risk her life in pursuit of her sister. She'd expected his rebuke, even punishment. So had her daughter Lamira, yet she'd chosen to act, anyway. They had succeeded in rescuing her elder daughter Lily, thanks to Zander's forced influence, and no one had been harmed. But they'd returned to the pod the night before and the time for the reckoning had come.

He fingered the leaf of one of Lamira's potted plants absently. "Yes."

She approached him, stopping a few feet away.

"You are my guest here, Leora."

"Yes, my lord."

"When I bought you, it was as a gift to Lamira. I have not made any demands of your service other than as her companion."

She dropped her head, sensing the rebuke that was coming. She had accompanied her daughter on an unauthorized, dangerous mission to rescue Lily, her other daughter. "Yes, my lord."

"As her mother, I would expect you to hold her health and well-being as the utmost priority. Even more so because she carries my young."

"Yes, my lord, that is why—"

"No," he cut her off. "Do not give me any explanation—I have no patience for your excuses. Allowing Lamira to risk her life as she did was unacceptable."

She kept her eyes trained on the floor. "Yes, my lord."

"You have displeased me, and I require that you be punished."

A knot tightened in her middle. Would Zander punish her himself? Lamira had suspected, when he'd first bought Leora, that he intended to use her, too, as a sex slave. How would her daughter react to hearing Zander had punished her?

A movement drew her attention to the doorway. Master Seke, the warrior, had been standing in perfect stillness. How long had he been there?

"I have asked Master Seke to punish you."

Her belly fluttered as Seke's blue-violet gaze held hers.

"As it seems you require a direct master, and it is inappropriate for me to take that role, you will now answer to him. He will take responsibility for you and your behavior."

She couldn't seem to breathe.

"Your obedience training begins today."

The prince's words rebounded in her head, ricocheting around like a rubber ball.

Your obedience training begins today.

Master Seke stepped forward from the shadows to claim her, his expression inscrutable. Like all Zandians, he stood taller than a human male, with purple-hued skin and two small horns on the top of his head. The Master at Arms' face was worn and scarred, and always composed. He moved forward to claim her with a feline grace that belied his size. His broad shoulders stretched the fabric of his tunic and a sword hung at his belt. Purple rimmed the blue irises of his eyes, which was unusual. The rest of the species she'd seen had brown-purple irises.

Against all reason, her pussy clenched at the mere idea of the scarred warrior punishing her. She'd always thought of him as *her* warrior, though they'd exchanged few words.

He placed a supple animal hide collar around her neck, caramel in color. It fit perfectly, snug but not bothersome. With a swift, easy movement, he gathered her hands behind her back and cuffed her wrists together with bands of what felt like the same supple leather.

His touch was impossibly gentle, considering the strength behind it. Just the brush of his skin against hers sent her flesh aflame.

Cuffing her was entirely unnecessary. She'd never win in a struggle against his species, and there were guards everywhere. Nor could she ever leave the Zandian's guardianship. They had knowledge about her past that would have her executed by the local species, the Ocretions, immediately. She could only assume cuffing her was for effect. To show his dominance, his mastery over her.

This male Zandian would soon punish her. Her sex tightened again.

He propelled her forward, his touch still light, but the direction plain.

How would he do it? Intimately? Or publicly? It would be physical punishment; she had no doubt. Lamira had intimated Zander spanked her.

In the factories where she'd met her human mate, Johan, and on the agrifarm where she'd raised their daughter Lamira and hidden her beauty from the greedy Ocretion masters, they'd used a shock-stick to keep the human workers in line. The pain from the shock was unbearable. Overuse caused permanent damage in the nerves and eventually in the brain.

But in the short time she'd been, as he put it, a *guest* on Zander's pod—since he'd bought her as a gift for her daughter, whom he loved—she'd seen no shock-sticks. There'd been no abuse. She and Lamira had always been treated with courtesy, even though it was understood they were slaves. They ate delectable food, slept in luxurious surroundings, and were not required to labor in any manner. Though her daughter wore a collar and cuffs, they were decorated with priceless Zandian crystals—part of the Zandian mating ritual, and she'd been well cared for here. Leora knew Zander punished Lamira, but it was privately. They hadn't spoken of it, but Lamira had never seemed to resent it. In fact, by her blushes, Leora suspected there was an enjoyable aspect to his mastery.

Was that why Seke was in charge of her? Had he *asked* to be the one to punish her? Since the very first planet rotation she arrived, he'd been solicitous with her, almost protective.

Was she to become Seke's sex slave?

The moment that thought tumbled through her head, she stumbled. Master Seke steadied her, slowing and showing a patience that again, seemed concerned. Something in her core pulsed with excitement, even as her mind rebelled. She stiffened her spine, preparing her resistance. Though she had little choice but to ultimately submit, that didn't mean she had to make it easy on Seke.

He led on, down a brightly colored corridor, the polished marble floors covered in expensive, hand-woven Ostrion rugs. Everywhere she turned, the opulence served as a reminder of the comfortable life she'd led there. This pod, no more than a giant spacecraft parked over Ocretia, was the sole seat of the Zandian kingdom until their species reclaimed their planet from the Finn.

He stopped before a door, which swished open when he placed his palm against the panel beside it. He pushed her into what had to be his chamber.

It was as beautifully appointed, as was every room in the palatial pod. An oval sleepdisk hovered on one side, suspended as if by magic. The thick mattress was draped in the finest fabrics of amber, green and midnight blue. Crystal-amplified light shone through a skylight, making the room, with its high ceiling, light and airy. A workstation hugged one wall.

But what made her breath stop and her solar plexus twist was the cage suspended in the corner. The punishment apparatus that stood on the bed. The tall basket filled with various manual implements, all designed to inflict pain.

A trembling started in her knees and traveled up her legs to her core. It turned her hands clammy and cold. To hide her terror, she lifted her chin and met the eyes of her new master. "So, am I to be your sex slave? I'm past the ideal age for breeding, surely you know that." At forty-one solar cycles, her body could still reproduce, but the risks were higher.

Something in Seke's face tightened, a slight strain showing beneath the marble mask. "No," he clipped. "You have displeased your host. Prince Zander ordered your punishment and training, but he gave his word to Lamira you would not be used as a sex slave."

She wondered if he inserted the part about the prince ordering it as a subtle means of letting her know this wasn't his own idea. Did he find it distasteful? She couldn't tell.

"Release cuffs." The cuffs, which had to be voice-commanded like the doors and locks in the pod, separated. "You will refer to me as *Master* at all times. You will keep your eyes lowered and your hands behind your back unless otherwise instructed. I expect your obedience and complete submission. Defiance will be immediately punished. Remove your clothing."

Even though she should have expected this treatment, his words struck her as if she'd been punched in the gut. From another male it would not have wounded so badly, but from Seke, the male who had always shown her such courtesy, it came as a betrayal. Before she could consider the wisdom of it, her hand shot out to slap him.

He moved even faster and caught her wrist, twisting it behind her back so she had to either spin around or have it wrenched in the socket. She whirled and he flattened her against the closed door, with one wrist pinned to her back, the other to the cool metal. Her cheek pressed against the door and his body covered hers, pinning her with the whole of his chest, his torso, the bulge of his cock against her lower back.

So. He did find this arousing. His hard muscles met most of her body, unyielding and warm.

The trembling in her legs grew stronger. "Seke," she whispered.

She didn't know what made her speak his name so intimately, as if they were lovers, not almost-strangers ordered by another to complete this strange scene.

And his breath was at her neck, hotter even than his flesh. "Defiance will be punished every time, Leora." He, too, sounded more like a lover than a keeper. She didn't hear anger, nor even danger in his threat. Only promise—sweet promise, as if he looked forward to conditioning her to his command.

She struggled then, terrified, not of the punishment, but of him and her body's reaction to him.

He took her hand from the door and folded it behind her back with the other one, fastening the cuffs together, once more. "Come." Again, there was no bark to his words, only quiet determination. He turned and guided her to the sleep-disk, where he sat and pulled her across his knees, her torso resting on the mattress.

She understood immediately what he meant to do, but held back from struggling. Perhaps, if she was honest with herself, she'd admit her curiosity, her fascination with the scenario—of being held so intimately on a male's lap to have a private part of her anatomy touched, punished by him.

When he pulled up her white robes, though, she came back to life, fighting against his obvious intent. Of course, her struggles were no match for him. He had only to scissor one leg over her kicking limbs to pin her in place. Her robes slithered up her back, the fine material sliding over her skin like a caress. The modest panties went in the opposite direction, down her thighs. He lifted his leg to wiggle them past it, and the cool air of the room hit her bare bottom.

She twisted, contorting her torso in an effort to bring her mouth to his arm to bite, but she couldn't reach.

The first slap of his enormous palm almost came as a relief—the actual punishment was better than the anticipation that had been twisting and coiling in her belly. Then pain bloomed and she started to fight anew. He spanked her fast and hard, a steady pace that covered every inch of the lower half of her buttocks.

Though she tried to keep her lips closed, not wanting him to know how quickly he'd conquered her, grunts and gasps slipped out and, at the loudest, he stopped and rested his paddle-like hand on her blazing skin.

Her back heaved with panting and she arched, lifting her head to protest the ignominious position.

"Tell me something, beautiful female, did you fight your Ocretion masters this way?"

Beautiful female. She wished his words didn't affect her, but she liked hearing the endearment far too well.

"No," she admitted after a moment.

Abruptly, his hand crashed down on her bottom again, slapping hard and fast.

She let out a mewl of protest.

"No, *master*," he corrected. "Try it again."

She stilled her struggles and closed her eyes. Something stubborn in her didn't want to give in, even though she knew she'd never win this battle.

As if he understood her every thought, he began spanking again. "You may keep resisting, little human, but I will break you in the end. And your punishment for displeasing the prince has not even begun."

Tears began to smart her eyes, not from the pain—the spanking wasn't light, but it wasn't unbearable—but from the humiliation.

"No, master!" she croaked angrily.

He stopped spanking, smoothing his rough, calloused palm over her twitching buttocks.

"Is this rebellion for me alone?" His words came softly, as much a caress as the hand circling her burning bottom.

Her heart thundered. Heat swirled in her core. She didn't understand his question, or the angle behind it, but the truth tumbled out before she could stop it. "Yes...master." Again, the tears burned.

And just like that, Master Seke righted her, letting her robes fall back down over her bared ass as he plopped her on his lap, one arm looped around her waist. Her panties were still lowered, tangled around her thighs, which kept her humiliation in place.

He rubbed his knuckles over her cheek and she resisted the irrational urge to lean into the touch. "This training was not my design, Leora." Regret echoed in the heaviness of his voice. "But it must be. You will humble yourself to me. I will punish you. And I will care for you, for that is the role of a master."

Her pussy clenched at the same time something twisted in her solar plexus. Desire at conflict with pride. Fear smeared around and between both. She almost wanted to give herself over to him, to let him punish and care for her.

Almost.

"Will I be allowed to see Lamira?"

"After your initial training, yes. Keeping you from her will be used as a punishment only—for both of you."

If this training was her fate, she wondered what punishment her daughter had met at her mate's hands. He'd be careful with her, because she carried his young. Even without the pregnancy, he'd be fair, though. She'd seen his love for Lamira.

Seke pushed her to her feet. "Release cuffs." The wrist cuffs sprang apart. "Remove your clothing. Being naked before me is part of your training."

Her eyes narrowed. "Why? I thought I was not to be used for breeding or sex."

He landed a swat on the back of her thigh. "I will tolerate your questions today because you are adjusting to the change in our relationship. In the future, I expect obedience without question. The reason I require you naked is to humble you."

Again, something twisted in her solar plexus and anger flashed. Her hands free, she lunged for his face, fingers curled into claws, aiming for his eyes.

He caught her wrists and one of his feet pushed the backs of her knees so she plunged forward. She gave a strangled cry that morphed into a groan as her knees hit the finely woven rug at his feet.

Seke's expression hadn't changed—his eyes glowed purple, but his face remained an inscrutable mask. He lifted her twisting hands to his face and stroked his cheek with them. She could have clawed his skin, could have inflicted that small wound, but her fascination with his action made her go quiet.

What was he doing?

"These hands," he murmured, still rubbing her fingers over his cheek, across his open mouth.

Was it her imagination, or had his horns stiffened and changed their angle—leaning toward her?

"These hands will learn to serve."

Enraged, she tried to pull them away, but while his grip wasn't harsh, his strength made it impossible. The next time he dragged her fingers across his mouth, he bit down—not hard—more sensually. Her eyes flew wide, heart stilled as she froze, staring up at him.

Shock danced over his features, as if he hadn't meant to nip her. His blue-violet eyes locked on hers and time stopped. The room spun. Desire throbbed between her legs as insistently as her bottom burned.

And then Seke released her. Suddenly. Violently. He tossed her hands down so hard they bounced in her lap and he stood, lifting one leg over her head. He moved away from her, toward the door, where he stopped and folded his arms over his massive chest, turning back.

"Stand. Disrobe. I am losing patience." His tone was much colder now—so unlike his usual courtesy, it wounded. And yet it made it easier to obey. This was a nameless, faceless master. Not her Seke. Just one of the hundreds of masters she'd had in her lifetime as a slave.

She clenched her teeth as she stood and pulled off her white robes, slid out of her tangled underpants, then stood facing him, hands neatly folded behind her back, as he'd instructed. She didn't lower her eyes, though. They both knew her submission wasn't genuine.

Something flickered behind his eyes. Pain or regret. He looked sickened, yet nothing on his expression had changed. Somehow, she read it, though. Perhaps it was the hint of instinct she had—that fraction of psychic ability her youngest daughter possessed in spades.

His throat worked to swallow. He scrubbed a hand over his face, then cleared his throat. "You will obey me."

She lifted her chest. "Yes, master."

READ ALL THE BOOKS IN THE ZANDIAN MASTERS SERIES!

His Human Slave (Zandian Masters, Book 1)

COLLARED AND CAGED, HIS HUMAN SLAVE AWAITS HER TRAINING.

Zander, the alien warrior prince intent on recovering his planet, needs a mate. While he would never choose a human of his own accord, his physician's gene-matching program selected Lamira's DNA as the best possible match with his own. Now he must teach the beautiful slave to yield to his will, accept his discipline and learn to serve him as her one true master.

Lamira has hidden her claircognizance from the Ocretions, as aberrant traits in human slaves are punished by death. When she's bought by a Zandian prince for breeding and kept by his side at all times, she finds it increasingly harder to hide. His humiliating punishments and dominance awake a powerful lust in her, which he tracks with a monitoring device on her arousal rate. But when she begins to care for the huge, demanding alien, she must choose between preserving her own life and revealing her secret to save his.

Read all the Books in the Zandian Masters Series!

~

Training His Human (Zandian Masters, Book 3)

"YOUR OBEDIENCE TRAINING BEGINS TODAY."

Seke has no interest in owning or training a slave. Not even Leora, the beautiful human who had captivated his thoughts and fantasies since her arrival on their pod. As the Zandian Master of Arms, he has a war to plan and new troops to train. He can't be tempted by the breathtaking human slave, who, according to Prince Zander, grows aroused by punishment. Yet he can't allow another male to bring her to heel either. Not his Leora.

In all her lifetime as a slave, Leora might have submitted in body, but never in mind. But the prince has given her to the huge, scarred warrior, Seke, for punishment and she finds he has unexpected ways of bending her to his will. Ways that leave her trembling and half-mad with desire. But her new master is unwilling to take a new mate, and she fears that once he deems her training complete, he will set her aside, leaving her heart in pieces.

~

His Human Rebel (Zandian Masters Book 4)

CONSCRIPTED BY AN ALIEN ARMY, SHE PLOTS HER ESCAPE...

Cambry doesn't believe the aliens' propaganda for one minute. The Zandians may have saved her from one death, but they planned to send her to another. She bides her time, waiting for her chance to get away and find her brother, enslaved by a different species. The only thing she didn't count on was Lundric, the tempting Zandian warrior who, for some reason, decided she was his female.

Read all the Books in the Zandian Masters Series!

Lundric knew the fierce little rebel Cambry belonged to him the moment he saw her toss that auburn hair in defiance. He knows she hasn't accepted him or the Zandian's cause, but he vows to win her, no matter what it takes. But when Cambry steals a ship and attempts to escape, even his harshest punishment may not restore the trust between them.

ALSO, CHECK OUT THE HAND OF VENGEANCE

~Winner, Best Erotic Sci-Fi, The Romance Reviews Reader's Pick Awards~

ON HIS PLANET, WOMEN ARE PUNISHED WHEN THEY DISOBEY...

Dr. Lara Simmons can handle difficult surgeries on the battlefield of a war-torn planet. She can even handle her capture by rebels who need her skills to save the life of an important figurehead. But she wasn't prepared for being stuck out in the wilderness with Blade Vengeance, the fierce tattooed rebel warrior with antiquated views of gender roles and corporal punishment. Dominant and unyielding, he doesn't hesitate to take her in hand when she disobeys his rules. Yet he also delivers pleasure--with a passion she's never before experienced.

Blade finds the doctor from Earth sexy as hell, especially when she's giving him attitude, but once he delivers her safely to headquarters, he pulls back from her allure. Known for single-handedly starting the revolution and freeing many of his people, his life is one of hardship, slavery and war. Going soft on a woman isn't part of his plan, especially with the final strike of the revolution so close. But when he sends Lara back to Earth to keep her safe during the upcoming battle, he inadvertently delivers her into enemy hands. Can he find and save her from the revolution he caused?

WANT FREE BOOKS AND SPECIAL DEALS FROM RENEE?

Go to http://owned.gr8.com to get *Owned*, a military BDSM novella. You'll also be signed up for Renee Rose's newsletter and receive free copies of *Theirs to Punish, Discipline at the Dressmaker, The Alpha's Punishment* and *Her Billionaire Boss* (written under her other pen name Darling Adams). In addition to the free books, you will get special pricing, exclusive previews and news of new releases.

FROM THE AUTHOR

Thank you for reading *His Human Prisoner*! If you enjoyed it, I would really appreciate it if you would leave a review. Your reviews are invaluable to indie authors in marketing books so we can keep book prices down.

OTHER TITLES BY RENEE ROSE

Sci-Fi

The Hand of Vengeance, His Human Slave, His Human Prisoner, Training His Human, His Human Rebel, Her Alien Masters (coming May 5th)

Dark Mafia Romance

The Don's Daughter, Mob Mistress, The Bossman

Contemporary

Theirs to Protect, Scoring with Santa, Owned by the Marine, Theirs to Punish, Punishing Portia, The Professor's Girl, Safe in his Arms, Saved, The Elusive "O" (FREE)

Paranormal

The Alpha's Promise, His Captive Mortal, The Alpha's Punishment, The Alpha's Hunger, Deathless Love, Deathless Discipline, The Winter Storm: An Ever After Chronicle

Regency

The Darlington Incident, Humbled, The Reddington Scandal, The Westerfield Affair, Pleasing the Colonel

Western

His Little Lapis, *The Devil of Whiskey Row*, *The Outlaw's Bride*

Medieval

Mercenary, *Medieval Discipline*, *Lords and Ladies*, *The Knight's Prisoner*, *Betrothed*, *Held for Ransom*, *The Knight's Seduction*, *The Conquered Brides (5 book box set)*

Renaissance

Renaissance Discipline

Ageplay

Stepbrother's Rules, *Her Hollywood Daddy*, *His Little Lapis*, *Black Light: Valentine's Roulette (Broken)*

BDSM under the name Darling Adams

Medical Play

Yes, Doctor, *His Human Vessel (coming soon!)*

Master/Slave

Punishing Portia, *His Human Slave*, *Training His Human*

ABOUT THE AUTHOR

USA TODAY BESTSELLING AUTHOR RENEE ROSE is a naughty wordsmith who writes kinky romance novels. Named Eroticon USA's Next Top Erotic Author in 2013, she has also won *The Romance Reviews* Best Historical Romance, and *Spanking Romance Reviews'* Best Historical, Best Erotic, Best Ageplay and favorite author. She's hit #1 on Amazon in the Erotic Paranormal, Western and Sci-fi categories and is a contributor to *Write Sex Right* and Romance Beat. She also pens BDSM stories under the name Darling Adams

Renee loves to connect with readers! Please visit her on:
  Blog | Twitter | Facebook | Goodreads | Pinterest | Instagram

ACKNOWLEDGMENTS

Thank you for great beta read from Katherine Deane.
And of course, thank you, readers for indulging my slave fantasy!

Printed in Great Britain
by Amazon